If I Could Be With You

Mary Mamie Hardesty

DEDICATION

For all my fellow readers out there who are in love with LOVE.

ACKNOWLEDGMENTS

Thanks to all my friends who gave advice and encouragement, in addition to all the writers from whom I've drawn inspiration and encouragement through the years.

PART ONE

CHAPTER ONE

He was married. Was there anything else that could be added to that sentence to make it OK? He was married, but unhappily? He was married, but to a bitch? He was married, but secretly gay? None of which were true, and yet, when he held her hand, and asked about her life, she felt like she was the only woman in the world. Dreams of his hands on her body, their weight as they covered her both safe and erotic, overwhelmed her.

She touched the numbers on her cell slowly, entering the New York prefix, knowing she had seven digits more before she had to make a choice. In this chess game of attraction it was definitely her move, but she had little experience with strategy. Just last week she had contemplated affairs with married men in the snobbish manner of a Puritan elitist. As her high school friend talked of her affairs, she'd laughed and nodded, but judged nonetheless. Now, she sat in a similar position.

The phone rang three times to voicemail. A sensuous, deep voice spoke, "This is Charles. You know what to do."

"Charlie, It's Hannah. I was just calling to make definite plans for the weekend. No hurry, since I'm not leaving until Thursday. Call back whenever."

She had set things up to stay with him before she'd seen him at the fundraiser for a local charity. She recalled Lilly's reaction at seeing Charles after his eight years away.

"My goodness. Did you see how good he looked? Those blue eyes and dark curls? God, I wish Joe still had hair! And don't even get me started on his backside. I'm sorry, but little Charlie McMillan is hot."

The sorry probably came from the fact that for most of their lives, Charlie had been too young to think of as anything but an annoyance. He'd been eighteen when he'd left for school, but they'd been women in their late twenties, intensely focused on marriage, not college boys. Lilly's quest had been successful, Hannah's – not so much.

She'd stared at him on the dance floor. He was hot. How could she have forgotten? It had made her all the more self-conscious of the fact that she'd already invited herself to stay at his place when she visited New York in a few weeks while taking professional development classes at Columbia. While saving money was certainly her intention and a plus, she'd also been looking forward to having someone to hang with that could show her around the city. Now her idea of hanging seemed to be evolving quickly into fantasies that made her slightly uncomfortable.

He'd been so gracious when she'd asked.

"Nadia went home to Morocco for two months. I have plenty of space, and a guest bedroom," he'd said.

She'd been filled with sisterly feelings of gratitude, feelings of gratitude that dissipated immediately at the party upon seeing his well-muscled torso and tight ass. She threw herself against her pillow and remembered the state of arousal she'd found herself in while sipping champagne from across the room. It had been foreign and exciting.

Her body had turned off after her breakup with Jess six months ago. No matter whom she met, or how she'd flirted, she was numb below the waist. The only thing working for her had been her favorite online site and her little friend in the bedroom drawer – and even those occasions had been rare. Desire had been a word sorely missing from her vocabulary for too long.

Charlie barely spoke of his wife that night. Whenever anyone brought Nadia up, he'd managed to shift the topic as he glanced her way. The air of confidence and maturity that oozed from him shocked her. He had casually touched her arm and back earlier in the evening, gradually progressing to her waist as he squeezed past her to the bar. Just a light touch, it could have been an accident, but the heat that rushed through her let her know she didn't want it to be.

"So what's going on in your life, Miss Hannah?" He'd reached out and taken her hand just as she'd realized the table at which they sat had emptied and only strangers sat a few yards away, engrossed in an intense conversation about the latest ecological disaster.

"The usual." She didn't know how much he wanted to know. They'd never been close. Their families had celebrated holidays and she'd given him hugs while surface talking for years but she'd sensed that night he was looking for more. Of course, that could have been the bubbly.

"Tell me."

"Well, it's almost summer so I'll be finished with work for a while. I need to decompress some and get a little professional development time in, that's why I'm headed to New York."

"Yeah, I'm really glad you're coming. The city's an amazing place. I'm looking forward to showing it to you."

"You know you don't have to do that. I don't want to impose. The room is plenty."

"Are you kidding? Hannah Miller in New York City and you expect me to stay in? I've wanted a chance to spend quality time with you since we were kids."

4

She didn't mention to him that they'd never really been kids at the same time. It was flattering to be complimented with such finesse. She laughed instead.

"Well then, you're welcome. If I'd known I was fulfilling a dream I'd have scheduled a flight years ago."

"Seriously," His thumb had stroked her palm. His hand was large and covered hers completely. "I can't wait to have you there."

She'd swallowed hard at his choice of words. It had flustered her enough to leave her speechless. She was out of practice, but she knew what it felt like to flirt, and be flirted with. What was he doing?

"How's your family?"

"Oh, they're fine. They're loving Phoenix. Mom golfs every day and Dad's still working hard at the bakery, but I think he's close to retiring."

At the mention of her father he'd flashed a broad grin.

"Glad he's not around tonight actually." He'd squeezed her hand and continued, "Did you know that when I was younger he told me if I ever touched his daughter, he knew ten ways to kill me?" He'd let his eyes linger on their tangled fingers.

"What? He must have been talking about Susie." She referred to her youngest sister that had been closer to Charlie's age.

"No, no. He was definitely talking about you. We'd all gone to the movies together, and I guess he caught me looking at you a little too intensely for his liking."

"Intensely? What are you talking about? You were like 10 years-old then."

"I've always been a man that knew exactly what he wanted Hannah."

She'd crossed and uncrossed her legs, quickly dropping his

5

hand as she saw Lilly making her way to their table. What would she say about the conversation they were having?

He'd turned to see what had changed and invited Lilly over to sit and relax with them. He did it with such ease that she wondered if she'd imagined it all. She'd seized that moment to make her retreat. As she'd leaned in to hug him, his lips brushed her cheek. The sudden blast of electricity between them could have sparked a city-wide blackout. She'd backed away and hugged her sister, explaining that she had to be somewhere early the next day.

That was three nights ago. She put her cell on the bedside table, and exhaled her pent up breath. In three more nights she would be sleeping in his apartment, the apartment he shared with his beautiful wife she'd met only once, and wouldn't be seeing this summer. Surely when she was in his home, the pictures and presence of another woman's things would bring her hormones back to reality. He'd been flirting, that's all, just flirting, and he'd done nothing wrong. But she wondered, had Nadia seen the way he'd held her hand at the party, would she have agreed?

CHAPTER TWO

Hannah loved the descent portion of a flight. Lilly and Susie found take off to be the most exciting, but she never felt safer in a plane than at landing. Bumps and all, the reality of being so close to her destination gave her the feeling of inevitable safety. She waited in her seat knowing that she could take her time as anxious passengers making connections rushed past her. No need to hurry, she was in a new place worthy of her attention.

LaGuardia airport surprised her in its simplicity. She wasn't sure what she expected but it didn't feel as if she was in New York City. She made her way to the baggage claim and into the taxi line before it finally dawned on her. She wasn't really in New York City, well not the New York City of the movies. That was Manhattan, or maybe the Bronx. She was in Queens, and it felt eerily similar to her hometown.

"Fifteen dollars," the heavily accented taxi driver said pulling up to a small building that apparently held Charlie's apartment. She counted out the cash, added a small tip, and gathered her belongings. When she turned to grab her bag she heard his familiar voice call her name. She has such a hard time reconciling the voice of a man with her memory of a boy.

"Hannah! I've been waiting." He reached out and took the bag from her hand, placing his free arm around her shoulder.

My God, he smelled good, clean and fresh with just a hint of summer sweat. The feel of his body pressed against her did nothing to alleviate the feelings of attraction that had been building since the night of the party. If he noticed, he didn't react. He ushered her into a small two-bedroom apartment sparsely furnished, but well kept.

"Sit down! Summer taxi rides from LaGuardia can be a heated endeavor. Let me get you a cool drink."

She sat on a comfortable loveseat next to an open window. There seemed to be no air in the apartment but a nice breeze found her, lifting her wet hair off the back of her neck. It had been a warm cab ride, and she could feel her clothing sticking to her curves. What she really needed was a cold shower, and not just because of the weather.

"Here you go. Tall glass of ice water. I've been holding off on the air for as long as I can. Not good to waste energy in today's economy right?"

She nodded, but totally disagreed. Air conditioning was a necessity in her life.

He sat and angled his body towards her, one arm on his leg and the other carelessly thrown against the back of the sofa. Was it her imagination or did the air between them actually crackle? He let his gaze drink her in without any effort to hide his appreciation. She drained the water from the glass and placed it on the table and looked around for a picture of his wife to calm her nerves and give her the strength to resist throwing herself at him, but there were no pictures in the room.

"We just moved before Nadia left for Morocco. There's a lot of stuff still in storage. Would you like the tour or do you need to sit a while longer?"

"Oh. I'm fine, really." Then she paused, felt her heart beating fast against her ribcage, and changed her mind. "Yes, give me the tour and I'll put my things away. I think if you don't mind, I'd also love a shower. Travel always leaves me feeling a little yucky."

"Sure."

He leaned over to grab her bag and took her hand in his, pulling her from the couch and not letting go as he led her to her room. It was strange to Hannah, this physical affection that seemed to naturally emanate from him. Perhaps it was really just who he was and she was reading too much into it. She decided to give him the benefit of the doubt.

"Here's your room. The shower's right in there and connects to my room, so you'll want to lock the door for privacy. I'm sure you don't want me busting in on you, right?" His eyes seemed to sparkle mischievously at the thought.

"Good advice! Thanks." She pulled her hand from his and opened the bag upon her bed trying to signal her readiness to be alone.

She pulled out her shampoo and conditioner and turned on the shower. When she had the perfect mix of warmth with a chill in the water she stripped her shirt from her body and removed the rest of her clothing piece by piece. A mirror covered the wall opposite the shower and as she undid her bra, she caught a glimpse of her hard rose-colored nipples. She couldn't help what she was feeling. It was like she'd been in a constant state of arousal since he'd confessed his boyhood desire in the yard. Her breasts were no longer the breasts of a sixteen year old girl, but they were full and perky, and her favorite part of her body.

She let her hands cup them as her fingers reached for her nipples and squeezed tightly. The pinching sent a shiver of pleasure straight through her. She saw the look of desire glaze her own eyes and she wondered how she would make it through these five weeks with her morals intact. She had no intention of sleeping with a married man.

She stepped into the shower and let the water trickle down her shoulders, rubbing it all over her breasts and stomach. She leaned against the wall and propped up her knee so she could cleanse between her legs, letting her hands follow the path of the water. As she did she imagined her hands were his, caressing her thighs. She let out a low moan and pressed her wet fingers against her center.

If she didn't find her release in the shower there would be no hope of holding back when Charlie was next to her. She rubbed herself in small circles and felt the tension mounting. She breathed in the scent of water mixed with her own wetness, and when she thought she couldn't handle anymore she let her finger pitch inside of her.

She knew the feelings of his hands on hers. It wasn't hard to imagine that her finger was his, sliding in and out, deeper and deeper inside of her while she pretended her thumb on her clit was his tongue.

"Oh God!" She gasped and came hard. Wave after wave of release pulsed through her.

The click of a door brought her crashing back to reality and she peeked round the shower curtain. Had she forgotten the lock? Oh my God. There were towels on the counter. Had there been towels on the counter when she got in the shower? She'd been so into her fantasy that she hadn't noticed.

What if he had heard her? How would she face him knowing he could have been a few feet from her when she came? Thank God she hadn't called out his name. She returned to the business of her shower, trying to wash away her embarrassment with the grime in her hair.

CHAPTER THREE

Hannah's first subway ride was an experience. The R train was packed with commuters making their way into the city for various evening escapades as they headed out to meet Charlie's friends at a Mexican place in Greenwich Village. With nowhere to sit, she ended up holding onto the hanging bar with one hand. When the car lurched forward, she fell back against him and found herself wrapped in his free arm. She thought she could make out the feel of his arousal against her backside and tried to think of anything else. Could anyone around them see what was going on? Would they even care if they did?

"You'll be a pro in no time. It just takes some getting used to," he said as he let his hand rest on her hip. She felt his even breathing on her neck. Her fantasy in the shower flashed through her mind. To distract herself, she took in the diverse nature of the passengers. Conversation in languages other than her own surrounded her. Nothing in her experience of small town Ohio compared. She felt an excitement and a strange affinity with the whole experience. This was exactly what she had hoped the subway would be. From the loud and obnoxious, to the quiet readers, no one was afraid to go about their own lives. They weren't even paying attention to her.

"So, where are we going and who are we meeting?"

Charlie had been pretty private regarding their plans.

"Mexican food and friends from college. You'll love it and the Village...promise."

When they emerged from the subway into the fading evening sun, Hannah felt deep contentment stir in her chest. This was the home she'd been looking for her whole life. The noise from the traffic, horns blaring, the smells - some good and some not, all of it felt like it fit. She looked up at the buildings, not skyscrapers as she'd expected, but still taller than what she'd grown up around.

"And you went to college here?" Her voice filled with awe. "What an amazing life you must have had." She was almost jealous. Her hometown experience of college life had been filled with good times, but who could she have become here in this metropolis?

Charlie grabbed her hand, leading her through the throngs of people moving purposely towards their goals: families, dates, work, parties, an end of the day drink. Who knew what the evening held in store for any of them? After a short walk down tree-lined streets that seemed straight out of a film, they came across an open-air patio with patrons drinking margaritas amidst Latin music. With happy hour just beginning, they were lucky enough to get a table for four by the sidewalk.

"Two passion fruit margaritas and some chili rellano. Does that sound alright to you, Hannah?" But the waiter had already turned from them. He'd just asked to be polite.

Part of her immensely disliked that he had ordered for her. Another part of her was enjoying this younger man that was so obviously in control of every part of their time together. If he was really that in control, it might not matter what she wanted when it came to sleeping with him, whether her decision was yes or no.

"You'll love these margaritas. They were the first drink I fell in love with in the city. We've been coming here for years. I love being able to share it with you."

"Do you bring Nadia here?" It was out before she could stop it. She'd expected discomfort, but received blasé at best.

"No, Nadia doesn't drink. She's Muslim, you know."

No, she didn't think she had. Had she ever had a reason to wonder? It wasn't like she'd been pining after him for years. His life between leaving Ohio and up until last week had been a mystery to her. She vaguely remembered wedding photos at a Christmas party, but they were at a park, nothing overtly religious.

He deftly stayed relevant, but moved the subject away from Nadia. "Have you ever dated outside of your faith or race?"

It was an interesting question. One he seemed intellectually curious about, like he wanted to discuss the idea philosophically, rather than personally. She'd begun to notice that habit in his conversation. He would ask a highly personal question, yet proceed to discuss it from his viewpoint as if it were a case to be studied.

"I have." She didn't want to be studied.

"Tell me about it," he reached across the table, again taking her hand.

"I'd rather talk about you and whether you've always been so physically affectionate. Is it with everyone, or just me?"

He smiled as if he'd been caught at something, but kept his hand on hers.

"A little of both, I think." He paused and looked into her eyes, "What did you want my answer to be?"

"I don't honestly know." Emboldened by his gaze she continued, "If you said you were like this with everyone, it would take away the thrill of not knowing your intentions. If you said it was just for me, the clarity of your intentions would scare me."

He raised her hand to his lips, not kissing it, just holding it there, as if lost in thought. The waiter sat two icy orange concoctions in front of them and he released her to partake of the drink. They sipped quietly, neither knowing what the other might be thinking. Just as she was becoming uncomfortable, a feminine voice rang out from across the street.

"Charles!"

A short curvy woman in her mid-twenties crossed through traffic next to a hippie looking man who had to be at least forty.

"Melanie! Eric! Come on over. We've saved you seats."

The couple made their way through the crowded patio and sat down with Eric next to Hannah, and Melanie next to this man she called Charles instead of Charlie. The flash of jealousy felt ridiculous. Melanie and Eric were obviously a couple, despite the large age difference. Why should she care who sat next to whom?

"I'd love for you both to meet the object of my teenage fantasies, Ms. Hannah Miller. Hannah, this is Eric Low and Melanie Highstreet."

Melanie held out her hand and gave Hannah's a quick squeeze.

"I heard all about you in college, Hannah. I feel like we've already met."

Hannah looked quickly to Charlie to see if this was a secret just spilled, but he didn't seem embarrassed or uncomfortable. He simply smiled.

"I can't imagine that Charles would have had much to say back then." She used his grown-up name.

He winked at her and casually moved the conversation along.

"How was your trip to Vermont?" He directed the question to Eric, but Melanie answered while Hannah sat back and sipped continuously on her margarita. The vigilant waiter brought her another, and another, as she listened to the threesome's shared journeys.

"I think when I retire I'd like to live in Vermont, definitely someplace rural and away from the city," Charlie said.

"But it's so amazing here, why would you ever want to leave?" Hannah finally had the courage to jump into the conversation.

"I love the energy here, but at some point in my life, I'd like to slow down, find that peace that you can only get when you are surrounded by nature, you know?"

He was looking at her with a dreamy gaze that made his youthfulness all the more apparent. What was she doing with this kid? He was talking about a retirement that was at least eight years further off than her own.

Melanie interrupted her thoughts, "So Hannah, you're a teacher? That must mean you get lots of travel time. How is it that you've never been to New York before?"

"Teaching isn't as profitable as you might imagine," she laughed. The margaritas were definitely easing the tension of making small talk with strangers. "I've been paying off student loans for years so I haven't managed too much traveling yet. But it's on my list." She smiled at Charlie as she felt his foot nudge hers below the table. Accidental? She was definitely buzzed and wasn't sure she cared.

"I hear you with the student loans! If I hadn't found my sugar daddy here," she reached over and rubbed Eric's bald head, "I'd be in a shelter for sure. Social work isn't as profitable as you would imagine either." She laughed and leaned back in her chair.

"That's what I'm here for darling," Eric dead-panned. "To fulfill your every monetary need and desire. Among other needs and desires…" His eyes took on a wicked gleam and she heard Melanie sigh.

Had she been sober, she might have started to feel a bit uncomfortable, but as it was, the feeling of Charlie's knee pressed against hers under the table was unbearably arousing. She knew she should stop the flow of margaritas, but she was on vacation and she so rarely had any fun anymore. Surely she could trust him to stop her from crossing any lines.

Before she knew what was happening, Melanie stood and reached for Eric's hand.

"It's been a fabulous night and it was so good to finally meet the infamous Hannah," she said as she held out her hand. "I'm sure I'll see you again before you leave."

Hannah shook it and did the same with Eric and the two turned and disappeared through the crowd.

"Lovely to meet you, Hannah," Eric called as he let himself be pulled off.

Charlie looked at her. "Well, that was subtle."

"What do you mean?"

She had been so lost in her own inner conflict about being half drunk that she hadn't picked up on anything else around her.

"They obviously wanted some alone time." He winked.

"Oh…oh!" She giggled in a way she only did after one too many drinks. When she heard herself she knew there was no going back. She was drunk.

"I take it you're enjoying the passion fruit?" he asked as his hand brushed her knee, definitely on purpose.

"I am," she reached across the table and took his other hand, brave from the drinks and the fact that they were alone again. "I'm also enjoying the fact that Melanie seems to have heard about me before. Why did you talk about me in college so much?"

He let go of her hand to pay the bill, then immediately reclaimed it.

16

"I've already confessed my school boy crush, Hannah." He smiled a devastatingly handsome smile. "I've compared every woman in my life with the image of you."

She sat in stunned silence. That was as close to as an actual confession of desire as he'd ever come with her. She knew in that instance, married or not, he was hers for the taking if she wanted him. But did she really want him?

She let her eyes roam his hard jaw and the muscles of his neck that flowed into his broad shoulders. His honey skin caught the glow of the candle on the table as his dark wavy hair blended in with the night sky. His lips were slightly parted and he stared at her with such intensity that she suddenly realized she'd stopped breathing.

"I'm a confident man, Hannah, but I'm not used to being left hanging after a confession of that magnitude."

She shook her head to clear it.

"Restroom?" she asked as she stood, holding onto the table for balance.

"Through the double doors on the left."

He looked disappointed. She shouldn't have had that last drink. Her head wasn't clear and her hormones were going crazy. She didn't want to do anything she would regret tomorrow.

Inside the restroom she splashed cold water on her face and readjusted her make-up. She would return to the table and act as if nothing had happened. She'd suggest they head home since they had a long sightseeing day planned in the morning. If she gave into temptation now, the trip would be ruined. Her guilt over sleeping with him would never let her stay the remainder.

He was waiting for her when she came out.

"Are you alright?" He took her hand and led her into the streets of Greenwich Village. "I should have warned you about

17

those margaritas. They sneak up on you."

"Kind of like you?" she said without thinking.

He stopped and looked at her, head cocked questioningly to the side.

"I guess so. How did I sneak up on you Hannah?" He pushed a strand of her hair behind her ear, leaving his finger to linger at her jaw. The way he looked at her made her body ache with need. She wanted him to kiss her.

"When I made my plans to come here I never thought I would be this attracted to you." She was shocked at her own alcohol-induced honesty. She searched his eyes for a response. They darkened with desire.

"I've waited my whole life to hear you tell me you want me, Hannah. I just wish you didn't have to be drunk to say it."

"I am drunk. I am, but I want you and I've wanted you since the night of the party. When you're close to me, my body goes haywire. I'm on fire and I can barely catch my breath."

His thumb caressed her bottom lip and she tilted her head.

"Will you still want me when you're sober?" he asked.

Why, oh why wouldn't he just kiss her?

"I will still want you forever," she whispered. "But when I'm sober, I'll be painfully aware of how very married you are."

He laughed at that. She found it odd that he could place so little value on his marriage. Could she actually be attracted to a man that could cheat on his wife? She felt his hand fall from her face and he put his arm around her to guide her towards the subway.

"Come with me, Hannah. We'll put you to bed – alone – and then we'll have a chat in the morning. If your head doesn't hurt too much."

She didn't know what had happened. One minute she was teetering on the edge of desire and the next she was embarrassed and being walked home by a much younger man who was acting like a big brother! Damn alcohol. She just shouldn't drink.

CHAPTER FOUR

Hannah awoke to a mouth that felt as dry as a desert.

"Water," she managed to rasp as she opened one eye to survey the room around her. Light blue walls reflected the morning sunlight and she squinted in pain. On the nightstand next to her sat a full glass of water and a bottle of ibuprofen. A handwritten note with a smiley face read, "Take me."

She sat up to reach for the bottle and was startled to feel the cold air against bare skin. She ran her hand down her totally naked body. She had no memory of taking off her clothes or getting into bed. Had Charlie helped her? Did anything happen between them? Surely she would have remembered kissing him. Kissing - that triggered something.

No, there had been no kissing. She'd embarrassed herself. He was going to kiss her and then she'd brought up his wife. In the long run it was probably for the best. While a drunken night of hot sex with a much younger, amazingly gorgeous man would have been a dream come true, her integrity was probably more important.

The door opened and she pulled the covers to her breasts.

"Good morning, Hannah!" Charlie was carrying a tray with fruit, bagels and steaming hot coffee.

Her stomach lurched at the food but her pounding head told her the coffee was a no brainer.

"Did you sleep OK?"

"Umm, I honestly don't know. Do you happen to have any idea how I ended up naked?" She eyed her neatly folded clothes on the chair in the corner.

"I do." He winked at her.

"What happened?" She covered her eyes with her hand, peering out from between two fingers.

"Don't worry. Your honor's intact. You didn't sleep with a married man or anything," he teased. "You were so drunk when I brought you in here that you started taking things off and throwing them on the floor before I could even look for your night clothes. I picked everything up and put it on the chair, made sure you were covered up and let you be."

"Ah. Oh my God. I'm Sorry, Charlie." She shifted her position under the covers. "I'm so embarrassed."

"So we're back to Charlie," he said.

She looked around the decidedly girly room, trying whatever she could to avoid his gaze.

"Don't be sorry. It was quite a show. I thoroughly enjoyed watching your unintentional striptease."

As if she wasn't uncomfortable enough with the headache and raging thirst, he had to continue last night's flirtations? She needed to put a stop to this sooner rather than later but before she could say what was on her mind, he'd set the tray down and quietly closed the door behind him.

Hannah took the ibuprofen and a long hot shower before lying down for another few minutes. When she got up she finally started feeling like herself again. Unfortunately, she was also starting to feel supremely awkward. She entered the living area with the intent of hashing it all out.

They were grown-ups. There needed to be ground rules. There

were some lines she wasn't going to cross. She was surprised to see him sitting in the middle of the floor surrounded by photos. He patted the ground next to him.

"Come here. We need to talk."

"We do."

She sank to the floor beside him. He'd obviously showered after she did because small beads of water clung to the back of his dark brown curls. He pushed them behind his ear. Here we go again she thought as her body began to respond to the proximity of his. She felt warmth bridging the space between her legs and her breathing hitched.

He reached out and laid a casual hand on her thigh, absentmindedly rubbing his thumb lightly against the hem of the cotton shorts she'd picked for the day.

"Here." He showed her a picture of Nadia and himself from what looked like their college years. "I want to explain something to you and I need you to have an open mind," he said. "I know that from the night of the party you've been aware of the fact that I want you."

Her body betrayed her and reacted to his words despite the picture of his wife in her hand. She was a terrible person. She let the picture fall to the ground and noticed all the others. Nadia and Charles playing soccer, hanging out with friends, in caps and gowns at their graduation, it was obvious how much their lives intertwined.

"I don't think we should be talking about this."

He laughed.

"Stop it, Hannah! Let me get this out. We have to get it all out in the open to move forward."

So he wanted to put it all behind them as well. Her heart fell a bit, but she knew it was for the best.

"Hannah, you don't understand who Nadia is to me."

"She's your wife. What's not to understand?" She started to shift away, but his hand grabbed her thigh, harder this time.

"She's my best friend. She's been my best friend since I came to New York. I would do anything for her. Anything."

"I get it. You love her and you're married and we need to ignore whatever is happening between us because it can only lead to more hurt for everyone involved."

"For an older woman you aren't very wise." He smiled and took her hand.

"What?" She tried to pull away, but he refused to let go.

"She's my best friend. F-R-I-E-N-D. That's all she is and all she's ever been to me."

Hannah let the words slowly sink in. She became even more aware of how close he was sitting. A wave of anticipation rolled through her stomach.

"What?" she asked again.

"Nadia is my wife in name only. I married her because I love her – as a friend – and I couldn't let her be forced to leave the country."

Suddenly everything clicked into place. Nadia's absence at family events over the years, the girly room she was sleeping in, the fact that he was alone while she was in Morocco. His marriage wasn't romantic.

"I need some air."

Hannah stood and walked to the window. She leaned out taking slow deep breaths. Charles walked up behind her and placed his hands on her hips as he tugged her backwards. His strong hands turned her to face him, pulling her forward before his mouth crashed down on hers.

She couldn't catch her breath. Her lips parted and his tongue pushed its way inside while his hand buried itself in her wet hair. He pressed her back against the wall and moved his mouth to her neck where he bathed and sucked her sensitive skin. Tiny flames of desire licked at her and sent chills through her body wherever his lips trailed. She let out a groan of need so loud that it would have embarrassed her if her rational mind could have engaged, but all she could do was feel and say his name, "Charlie."

At the sound, his own moan escaped and he guided her down to the couch. When he lowered his body to hers, she felt the full length of him pressed upon her. His hard cock strained against his jeans and she could feel how large and ready he was for her. She let her hand push up against his chiseled chest and dragged his T-shirt over his head. Their eyes met and she could see the hunger that burned there. This man wanted her and knowing it only made her wetter with desire.

He moved his hand to the band of her shorts undoing the button and zipper, letting his hand slide in between the cotton undies and her hot skin. She heard him whisper, "Oh my God," as his finger slid into her slippery desire. "You're so wet. Tell me you want me, Hannah. Tell me how much you want me inside of you."

He rubbed his fingers over her clit setting her on fire with need. She tore her mouth from his.

"I want you. I want you deep inside of me. I've never wanted anyone the way I want you right now." She pushed her body harder against his palm. "Put your fingers in me!" She gasped out a "please" as he pushed his long fingers into her waiting pussy. He moved them in and out while she circled against his hand and felt her shallow breathing quicken.

"Oh God," she screamed as she felt herself on the edge of coming, "Oh God, Charlie, don't stop." He moved his fingers deeper inside and kissed her harder. She bucked forward into his hand as the waves of her orgasm overtook her.

"Charlie! Yes, yes, I'm coming." She pressed into him one last time before he slowly brought his fingers out from between her thighs.

"You are incredible," he whispered as her kissed her gently.

She looked into his blue eyes and saw nothing but desire. How had she gotten this lucky? She could still feel his swollen dick pressed against her thigh and she wanted nothing more than to make him come as hard as she had.

She scooted over and pushed him under her. Straddling him on the couch, she moved lower and unbuttoned his jeans. When she slid them from his hips, his cock sprung free and she was happy to see it was as impressive on sight as it had felt.

She leaned forward taking him first in her hands, moving them slowly but firmly up and down his shaft. She heard his sharp intake of breath and knew that he was enjoying himself. When her lips slid over the tip of him, she felt his hands in her hair and he spoke softly, "Oh yeah, baby, please. Please. Suck me harder, Hannah." She let her tongue swirl beneath the head of his penis as she followed his directions.

She was in control now. He wanted her and she had the power to give him this. Her hands moved in time with her mouth and she could feel him hot beneath her fingers, she could feel the desire straining to be set free as she continued to suck and flick. His hand tightened in her hair and she knew he was close.

"Hannah. Oh God, you're gonna make me come….ahhh." She felt him pulse with release and tasted him in her mouth. She swallowed and pulled back. Their eyes met, and they both knew that the desires they had momentarily sated had only started kindling.

"I can't believe this is happening," she said as she slid up into his arms.

"Believe it," he said as he kissed her forehead.

CHAPTER FIVE

Her eyes were closed but she was moving. No, wait. She was being carried. She opened her eyes and recognized the grey walls of Charlie's room from her tour the day before. His strong arms put her gently on his bed.

"Hi," she whispered while he lowered himself next to her, never breaking eye contact.

He let his hand trail from her cheek, down her neck, to her breast where he teased her nipple through the soft ribbed cotton.

"Hi."

Hannah felt her body begin to respond again. The quiet of the room and the warm laziness of the afternoon mingled with the scent of him to create an atmosphere of seduction that made every cell in her body vibrate. She watched him watching her. His fingers tugged and caressed her nipple. She'd played with that same nipple while she imagined being with him just yesterday. Had this morning really happened? Did he really tell her his marriage was a sham?

He lifted her shirt and ran his fingers inside of her bra pushing it out of the way just enough for him to lower his lips to the raised bud. His teeth softly scraped before his lips latched tightly around her and he alternated between sucking and licking. She reached beneath to undo her clasp and free herself for his kisses. He laughed and moved up to her neck snaking his tongue from her jaw to her ear.

"I guess you're up for round two?" he asked.

She pushed her fingers through his hair and turned his face to hers.

"I'm not sure we've completed the first round, Charlie."

She placed her lips on his and deepened her small kiss into one that left them both breathless. Leaning over she pushed his shoulder to the bed and threw her leg over his waist.

"First things first. The pants need to come off."

Before she could reach any lower he had already shimmied his jeans to his ankles. She reached back and dropped them to the floor.

"I'm liking the lack of underwear Mr. McMillan."

"Anything for you, Hannah." He smiled and her heart melted. She was in trouble. "But," he continued, "you have me at a disadvantage ma'am."

His hands unbuttoned her shorts and she rose up for him to pull them from her hips. She placed her hands on both sides of his head and lowered her lips to his neck as she rubbed her wet pussy over the length of his cock.

"I don't think so, not yet," he said and flipped her onto her back in one smooth movement. He began sucking her nipple while letting his hand wander between her legs, moving his fingers lightly over her and making her hips arch in need.

"You're killing me, Charlie. I want you so much."

He lifted his head and brought his lips to hers while parting her legs with his knee to move himself between them. She felt the tip of his hard cock as it pressed against her and all she could think was what it would feel like to have him all the way inside of her, to be filled with him. She lifted her hips begging him to enter but he just raised himself and his eyes roamed her face.

"If I'm never here again, I want to remember this moment," he said.

"Why wouldn't we be here again, Charlie?"

She raised her hands to his jaw and guided his mouth back to hers, muffling her moan of pleasure and relief while sinking into her. She could barely control herself and moved her hips in unison with his. Running her hands down his back she squeezed his firm, gorgeous ass and pushed him deeper inside until there was nowhere else for him to go. Delicious desire coursed through her body and threatened to take her to a place of oblivion. She was already beyond words.

"You're so wet and tight," he gasped as he picked up his pacing and pressed his lips against hers.

She breathed in his every exhale and rocked against him, each stroke deepening the yearning for release as it built in her core. She felt his body shift and he pulled her up.

"Now, you can be on top," he said.

She stretched her body upwards and reached down taking his dick in her hands as she guided him into her.

"Oh my God," she groaned as the new angle of his thrust sent shivers up her spine. She raised and lowered her body again, squeezing her muscles around him as she moved. Each thrust hit her in exactly the right spot and she felt herself building to climax.

"I want you to come," he whispered.

She threw back her head and rode him with no thought of what she looked like, no thought of what was happening between them, no care in the world except the pleasure that his body was giving her. When she felt his palm slide up against her clit she knew that coming was inevitable. She felt her body begin to shake and her hips jolted with each pulse of the orgasm that seemed to roll on and on.

She collapsed onto his chest and he rolled her to the side, slowly moving inside of her again. She caught her breath and began to match the rhythm of his strokes. She heard his breathing get faster and she knew he was close. She pushed back into him, taking him deeper inside, and felt a small tug of satisfaction when he came with her name on his lips.

CHAPTER SIX

"I can't believe I'm finally here." Hannah said as she admired the view of Central Park from on top the Metropolitan Museum of Fine Arts. "It looks so familiar, like I've seen it all so many times before."

"You have. It's in movies, the morning news shows, even from the plane when you flew over. It's crazy how something you have seen a million times before can be so new and overwhelming when you see it from a different perspective," he said.

"Hmmm. Are we talking about my view of the park or my view of you, Charlie?"

"Maybe both." He ran a hand over her shoulder, down her arm and laced his fingers with hers. "Had enough culture for today?" he asked, and led her back to the elevator and out of the museum.

"Never! Isn't a Broadway show next on the list?"

He frowned, "Slow down, Hannah. You'll have done the whole city in one week. What would we do with your other three?"

She pulled him to a stop, stood on tiptoes and kissed him lightly on the lips.

"I'm sure we wouldn't have a problem coming up with things."

"Things could be good." He smiled and kissed her in return. "But," he pushed her backwards and turned to keep walking, "I have an honor bound duty as your tour guide to make sure you are exposed to as much of New York City as possible. My Queens apartment can't be your only stop."

"You're the one who didn't want to see a show!" She stated flatly, stung by his rejection.

"I just said slow down. I already have tickets for us to see a show in a few weeks. I was hoping to indulge in a little tourist action this evening and show you Times Square."

"Oh, well, I guess that's OK then."

"You guess?" He grabbed her hand and pulled her along the taxi-lined path that led into the park. Everywhere she looked people were lounging or playing. Couples walked holding hands. Children shrieked. Runners ran in large groups.

A few yards to her right stood a man near a fountain waving something in the air. As they walked closer, she could see it was a giant wand that he used to create bubbles. Massive bubbles at least two feet in diameter danced on the breeze that drifted through the air.

"That's so cool," she said and stopped to watch as children came forward to try.

Hannah felt Charlie's eyes on her. His gaze made her skin tingle. How could it be that just yesterday she'd been so sure she would never touch this man and now she couldn't stand to be out of his reach? Of course, had he not confessed to marrying Nadia in name only, their experience today would be very different.

"Charles?" she asked as they started to walk again. "Does Nadia know about me?"

"Do you mean does she know who you are or does she know we're together?"

Seeing his brows draw together made her nervous. She suddenly felt like she didn't know as much as she thought she did.

"Both," she said glancing at his profile while he continued looking straight ahead.

"Nadia had already left for Morocco by the time you invited yourself to stay with me," he teased. "So, no. She doesn't know you're here or that we're together, but she absolutely knows who you are."

Hannah didn't know how to respond so she stayed thoughtfully quiet. It was understandable that she didn't know about her visit. Who knew how often they spoke? Perhaps it just hadn't come up in conversation. But surely, if Nadia knew who she was, then he would have mentioned her had they talked. If their marriage were truly one of convenience it wouldn't be any problem.

"So you haven't talked to her since she left?" she asked.

"No, I have."

What was he holding back? Why didn't his wife and best friend know about her visit if she knew about her existence?

"I don't understand. How could my month long visit not come up in discussion?"

"Hannah," he ran his hand through his chocolate curls, slightly sweat dampened by the heat of the afternoon sun. "Nadia's a little sensitive when it comes to you. I didn't want to make her uncomfortable or insecure, especially since I really had no idea that any of the 'things' that happened between us would even happen." He smiled.

"But," she started.

"I wanted them, yes. I've always wanted them, but I never in my wildest dreams thought you would want me back."

"You seemed so sure of yourself," she said.

"Well, I'm a man," he laughed. "I'm always going to try and make you believe that I can do what I set out to do."

Hannah looked down at their hands wrapped around each other. They fit. Years of holding hands with the wrong man made it feel that much more obvious when you found the right one, but the right one also happened to be wearing a wedding band. She decided to probe a little further.

"Why is she so insecure? I thought you said you were best friends."

"We are, but Nadia is used to being my only best friend. I've never really dated anyone seriously so she's never had to handle me having feelings for someone. The thought that someone might take her place in my life or that I might actually fall in love scares her a little. And," he looked Hannah straight in the eyes, "I get that and respect it."

Hannah took a deep breath, "So, what you're really saying is that while you consider your marriage to Nadia helping a best friend out, she has unreciprocated feelings for you?"

He stopped walking and pulled her down to sit next to him on a bench in the shade.

"I don't want to confuse things between us, Hannah. Her feelings at this point aren't important. Do you even know how you feel about me? Have you considered if you want me in your life beyond a summer fling? I have a life here and Nadia's a part of that. I'm not going to make her needlessly insecure or bring up painful conversations only for you to decide you don't want a younger man or New York, and head back to Ohio."

She leaned forward and put her hand to her forehead. How did she get herself into these situations? Why hadn't she brought all of these things up before she'd gone to bed with him? He had a point. Was he just a summer fling? Could she really see a future with him, and if she couldn't, was it fair of her to mess up what he had going on with Nadia - even if it was only friendship on his side?

She stood and held out her hand to him.

"Too much to take in today, Charlie. I don't have any answers for you."

"I'm not the one asking for answers...unless maybe it's to the question, 'Are you hungry?'"

"Starving," she said, and this time she was truly thinking about food.

***

As they boarded the train back to Queens, Hannah leaned on Charlie's shoulder and let the cool air engulf her. For a June evening, the city was particularly warm and the subway car offered a welcome respite. Charlie placed his chin on the top of her head as she played with the ring on his finger.

"What would you say about taking this off? At least until I leave in a few weeks?" When he didn't answer right away she continued. "I think I'd like to be able to consider how I feel about you and if this could be more than just a summer consummation of a teenage fantasy. It would help me to be in the same position as Nadia. I'd like to pretend she didn't exist, just so I can deal with whether I have feelings for you apart from your marital status."

Charlie lifted his hand and slowly slipped the ring from his finger placing it in the pocket of his jeans. When he put his hand back down it was placed strategically high on her thigh.

The train lurched to a stop and a few passengers exited. Except for a sleeping young woman in the back corner with a book covering her face, they were alone. Charlie lifted her chin with his free hand and gazed into her eyes before brushing his lips against hers. She angled her body so she could wrap her arms around his neck to draw him in closer. A quick glance behind her let her know the young woman was still dead to the world, so when his hand slipped up the leg of her shorts she thought, "What the hell?"

It wasn't like she could control the response of her body to his touch. His warm fingers swept feathery touches over her goosebumps from chilled subway car air.

"Is this OK, Charlie?" She breathed in the clean scent of his aftershave and ran her fingers over the stubble already present again on his hard jawline. "I mean, aren't there cameras or something?"

He laughed, "I'd love to fuck you right here, Hannah, but the subway's kind of dirty and I don't mean that in a good way." He wiggled an eyebrow at her. "I like your adventurous spirit, though." He pulled her thigh towards him so her legs were spread open. His left hand was still under her shorts and his fingers splayed over her panties that were already wet with wanting.

"Why are you doing this to me?" She pushed her forehead into his shoulder and closed her eyes as she reveled in the feeling of intense pleasure building deep inside of her.

"Because I can." He trailed light kisses from her ear to her collarbone. "And, I want to." He slid a finger under her panties, pushing them to the side.

A low moan escaped, despite pressing her mouth against his chest as she tried not to cry out.

"Here's our stop."

Hannah felt like crying as his fingers left her. He grabbed her elbow to help her stand up. Her knees buckled slightly but he caught her and helped her through the doors before they closed on top of them.

The hot city air rushed over her again and she was acutely aware of the uncomfortable slickness between her legs. She felt self conscious and shy. What had she just let him do to her? And how could she be so under his spell that she would have fucked him right then and there on the subway, if only he'd let her?

She laced her arm through his and pulled him closer to whisper into his ear, "You better be planning on finishing what you started Charlie. I like to play, but I like games that end with a pay off."

"All in good time, Hannah. Since you're already in a mood," he cocked an eyebrow in the direction of her chest where her nipples stood out in tiny hard buds, "we could stop off someplace interesting to indulge in a little more teasing."

"If it means hopping back on the subway, I think I'd rather save it for another night. I'd be just as happy to fuck you in the privacy of your own home."

He moved his hand from her shoulder to her ass, giving it a quick squeeze. She jumped in surprise. "That can definitely be arranged."

The rest of the walk from the station to Charles' apartment was quiet. Hannah couldn't help replaying the moments in the subway car over in her head, which led to her becoming more and more aroused. Charlie's body pressed against her as they walked was an aphrodisiac in and of itself and she couldn't move her feet fast enough to get back to his place.

He put the key in the lock and pushed the door open. Cool air hit their bodies. Hannah grabbed his face in her hands.

"You turned the air on for me?"

Charlie nodded, a sheepish grin spread across his face. She pulled him forward and kissed him. His tongue roamed her mouth while her hands moved lower to the button on his pants. She popped it and pushed his pants down his thighs.

"Don't you want to make it inside the apartment, Hannah?"

"No, Charlie," she said. "I don't."

His cock rubbed against her stomach, hard and long. He raised her arms and pulled her T-shirt over her head before pulling the rubber band from her hair, releasing crazy waves. Digging his fingers in, he guided her face back to his, kissing her until her breath came in quick, pulsing pants.

She felt his hands leave her hair and move to her back where he unhooked her bra, releasing her breasts so that her nipples rubbed the cotton of his shirt.

"We need to be naked," she said.

She pushed off her shorts while he removed his shirt before she pushed him against the wall and started to go down on him. He pushed her back and shook his head.

"Oh, no you don't. Just because you're older doesn't mean you're in charge. I think there's been an unequal exchange in the oral sex department of our relationship, and if there's anything you can count on with a man of my generation," he said, "it's a firmly held belief in equality."

He pulled her naked body into the living room and placed her in the red, cozy, armchair. She sank in as he pulled her hips to the edge before placing himself between her legs.

"I've tasted you on my fingers. Now, I'd like to taste you on my lips," he said as he caressed the tips of her breasts with his fingers before inching his hands from her torso to her thighs. He began massaging her tired muscles that had walked all day, working his way from her knees to her hamstrings and quads before zeroing in on her inner thighs.

"I've been dreaming about eating you out all day, Hannah."

His frank speech brought her hands to her face.

"Don't," he pulled them away. "Don't go getting shy and nervous on me now. Here's what I want you to do with those beautiful hands," he said as he placed them on her chest. "Squeeze your nipples for me, Hannah. The way you were doing in the shower."

She sucked in a breath.

"You did see me!"

She started to move her hands back to her face but he grabbed them and moved them to her breasts.

"You were beautiful. It made me so hot. I wanted to take off my clothes and step in there with you, but I had no idea if you wanted me to. Please don't stop me now. Play with your nipples. Rub your hands over your tits for me."

She closed her eyes and did as he asked. She was embarrassed, that was true, but she was also more aroused than at any other moment in her life. He lowered his mouth to her stomach and let his tongue wind its way to her center, kissing and licking his way around her pussy, only moving to her clit when he heard her gasp his name in frustration. Once there, he rhythmically sucked and moved his fingers deep into her.

She couldn't control her hips rising to meet him. The feeling of his fingers stroking her had her holding her breath. She let it out in a sob when he quickened the pace of both fingers and tongue. It was like nothing and no one else before. He was doing things to her body, taking her to a level of pleasure so high it was almost painful. If she didn't come she thought she might die.

She heard him moan. Was it possible that he was getting pleasure from this, too? She opened her eyes and was fascinated by what she saw. His face glistened with sweat and her wetness and his eyes were closed as he kissed and sucked at her center. One hand fingered her while the other held his rigid shaft. She'd never watched a man touch himself like that before. The idea that eating her out aroused him so much that he had to touch himself filled her with a sense of pride. He must have sensed a change in her because he stilled and looked up. Their eyes locked.

"Please don't stop," she begged, never taking her eyes off his. "Let's come together."

She saw hunger flash in his eyes as he rubbed her clit harder with his tongue. He pushed another finger inside her, fucking her with almost his whole hand while she watched him moving up and down on his cock with the other. She felt the pressure building in her core and knew she was close.

"Oh God," she whispered. Then more loudly, "Charlie, make me come!"

Everything happened at once. It was as if his tongue on her clit and his fingers deep in her pussy were connected to her own fingers squeezing her nipples. She forgot to breathe as her body convulsed and she felt herself pulse tightly around his hand. In the haze of her orgasm she could hear him groaning and knew he was coming with her. When it was over, he laid his head on her stomach and held her hips with his hands.

"I don't know how I'll ever be able to let you go, Hannah."

CHAPTER SEVEN

Continuing education classes at Columbia were all that Hannah expected and more. Despite the long subway ride, she returned home each night those first weeks excited to share her new teaching strategies with someone and Charlie listened to them all like a trooper. One Thursday evening, after four long days of learning, he met her at the door with a glass of red wine and a single red rose.

"What's this?" she asked, putting her books on the table by the door. She ignored the wine and the rose and instead went in for a long, sensual kiss.

"No fair," he said when she came up for air. "I have my hands full."

"Not anymore." She smiled and relieved him of the wine, took a drink, and reached for the rose. She inhaled the sweet scent then looked him in the eyes. "I do not deserve this."

"The last few nights have been the best of my life, Hannah. A little wine and a rose don't even begin to add up to what you deserve."

She walked into the living area and noticed candles all around.

"Mr. McMillan, I smell a seduction."

"Then you need to get your sense of smell checked. This is what's called an evening of appreciation. If you're seduced as a side effect, I can't control that, but my only intent is to show you how very happy I am that you're here in New York."

She looked at the coffee table and noticed the bottle of wine next to a plate of olives and cheese. He took the wine and poured himself a glass and said, "Sit down, I want to hear about your day."

"You've heard about my day everyday. I assure you there's nothing new. Why don't you tell me about yours instead?"

"OK," he said while pulling her feet to his lap and removing her sandals. "How about a foot massage while I talk."

"No!" She yanked her feet away and tucked them under her body. "My feet are disgusting from all the walking I had to do today. I wouldn't let you touch them if you paid me."

"You really aren't used to a man wanting to take care of you, are you?"

"Please! Foot massages, wine, and roses? This isn't real life, Charlie."

"It can be," he said. The smile left his face. "Tell me why you don't think you deserve to be loved, Hannah."

She raised her wine to her lips and took a large sip. How had she managed to ruin the romance in less than five minutes? Of course he thought this could be real. He was twenty-six and in a fake marriage. When had he even been in a real relationship? Her mind went back to what he'd said about Nadia not being used to him loving someone else. Surely he'd dated women in college.

"How many women have you been with, Charlie?"

He shot her a sneaky grin.

"More than you're thinking, Ms. Miller. I promise."

"Well, it's a legitimate question. You've admitted you aren't in love with Nadia and that she isn't used to competition," she said

"True. She's not and I will say, I haven't really ever loved a woman I've slept with. The possibility of present company excluded, of course." He tipped his glass to her. "But that doesn't mean I haven't slept with women. Even with the women I didn't love, I showed them the decency of romance and good manners. Who have you been with that hasn't given you your basic rights in a relationship?"

She almost spit out her wine. Basic rights in a relationship? Were all younger men this idealistic? She reached for some cheese.

"Well, let me think about that. There was Thomas in my college years, David in the years after, and Robert in my mid to late twenties, and oh, yes, the man I spent the past five years with. What was the asshole's name again?" She paused for effect. "Ah, that's right. Jess." She popped an olive in her mouth.

"Bitter much?" He laughed and took a sip of his wine.

They sat on opposite ends of the sofa, full glasses in hand, staring at one another.

"Actually, yes. I am."

"Tell me about Jess. I want to know how he broke your heart so I might have a chance at fixing it."

"I don't want to ruin a perfectly good night of appreciation. I'd rather give you my feet to rub," she said.

"But I'd rather take a stab at finally getting to know you, Hannah. I only have a few more weeks. I know your body like the back of my hand, but you've been holding back on your mind."

"I have shared more teaching strategy with you..."

He cut her off.

"I want a real chance for us, Hannah. That can't happen if you won't open up."

She swallowed and put her glass on the table. He reached to refill it. She almost said no, but if she was seriously considering telling him about her relationship with Jess, she knew she'd need the extra liquid courage.

"I call Jess an asshole and he was, but I have to take some responsibility for how dysfunctional we were. I let him treat me the way he did."

The air in the room suddenly felt charged.

"Did he hurt you?"

"Physically? No. No, it was nothing like that."

She saw his shoulders relax.

"No, with Jess it was all mental. He broke my spirit and then broke my heart. I seriously believed at one point we were heading towards marriage and kids."

"And you want that?" Charles asked.

"I know I'm not supposed to say so, but yes, I do."

"Who told you that you weren't supposed to want a family?"

"Jess did. Not in so many words, but he never wanted to discuss it. I knew that if I brought it up we'd probably end up fighting. He kept saying he loved me, he just didn't need the pressure."

She realized she'd spread out and Charlie's hand was resting on her foot.

"That's one of the reasons it's so hard for you that I'm married," he said.

"One of them, yes." She let out a laugh. "The other being that it's just so wrong!"

He smiled and she felt his fingers stroking her inner sole.

"We both know my marriage isn't real. I can love you, Hannah," he said.

"But can you give me what Jess couldn't? Are you ready for that?"

"Ready for a family?"

"Yes," she said. "A family, a home...a real marriage?"

"With you," he said. "Definitely with you."

"I think you're letting your crush on me overtake your rationality. Have you thought about what happens to Nadia if you fall in love with me? If you marry me? You can't be married to us both."

"Nadia and I married straight out of college," he said.

"I vaguely remember seeing pictures passed around that Christmas. Lilly and I thought you were too young, but Susie called it romantic."

"What I mean is that Nadia's already a citizen. She was able to apply after we were married three years."

Hannah sat up and pulled her feet from Charlie's grasp. She put her wine on the table and placed her face in her hands, shaking her head.

"What? What's wrong, Hannah?"

"Are you serious? You have no idea what might be bothering me about what you just said?" She stood and walked around the room blowing out candles and turning on lights. "Charlie! You are married to a woman that you haven't had to be married to for...what? Over a year at least?"

"Two," he dropped his gaze to his feet.

"Two," she repeated. "You made it seem as if your marriage was only about keeping Nadia in the country. Obviously there's more to it if you're still married."

"Please, sit down. I can explain," he said.

"I'm not sure you can."

She walked into her room and shut the door. Falling onto the bed, she buried her face in the pillow.

**

45

A few minutes later he knocked.

"Go away. I'm tired," she yelled as she got up, grabbed her night shirt and went to brush her teeth. This time she remembered to lock the bathroom door on both sides.

She was exhausted. The week had flown by and she was suddenly faced with the realization she was really sleeping with the much younger boy next door, who also happened to be a married man. Whether he was in a real marriage or not, he'd made the choice to stay in it longer than he needed to and she couldn't help but wonder why? Did he have feelings for Nadia he wasn't acknowledging? Was he a coward that couldn't bring himself to leave a secure situation? Whatever his reasons, he'd been less than honest from the beginning. True, he had never outright lied, but he had definitely omitted some pertinent facts.

Would she have slept with him had she known the truth? That while his marriage started out as a sham, he'd stayed in it voluntarily? What if she hadn't come to New York? Would he even be considering separating from Nadia or would he have stayed in their arrangement forever? She knew he was the only one that could answer these questions, however at present she had no desire to be in the same room with him.

She rinsed her toothbrush then splashed water on her face.

"What are you looking at?" she asked the mirror. "It'll be better in the morning. You just need some sleep."

Sleep apparently wasn't on Charlie's agenda. She opened the door to find him waiting patiently, cross-legged in the center of her bed.

"I've been selfish and a coward. Is that what you want to hear?"

"What I'd like to hear is the truth, but I don't want to hear it now. I'm tired. Just leave me alone."

"Hannah, it's not even eight o'clock. It's still light outside for Christ's sake. Is this how you handled your arguments with Jess? Because if it was, I'm sure it was oh, so effective," he mocked.

"Charlie, it's been a long week. I am realizing that I really don't know who you are or what kind of situation I've walked into here. We just sat out there on that couch and discussed marriage and children and I've only been in your life for a week."

"You've been in my life ever since I can remember, Hannah."

She swatted his hand away as he reached to pull her onto the bed with him.

"Don't," she said. But when he reached out a second time she let him win. She sat on the edge of the bed, her back towards him until her body betrayed her. Wanting to be closer to him, she turned to see his face.

"The feelings I've been having for you since the night of the party at Lilly's are the strongest feelings I've ever felt. I don't know if they're real or if they're lust. I don't know if you really like me or if it's some fantasy that will fade away when you get over the novelty of getting what you've wanted so long.

He reached out and ran his hand down her cheek, stopping at her chin and tilting it towards him.

"I'm coming off a break up where my life and dreams were literally wrecked. Why would you even want to be a part of this mess?" she asked and waited for him to speak.

"You might not know what you're feeling, Hannah, and that's OK. You haven't had as much time as I have to decide. What I'm feeling isn't lust, although my body craves yours like an addict. What I'm feeling for you is the stuff real marriages and families are made from. Maybe I haven't lived my life up to now in a way that makes it easy for us to be together, but to be fair to me, I never expected you to reciprocate my feelings."

47

She started to speak, "But you..."

He put a finger to her lips.

"Shhh. Hannah, give me a chance. You asked me to take off my ring so you could see what it would be like to pretend I'm not married. I did. Can you keep pretending? I promise in the grand scheme of our life, my marriage isn't anything we can't handle."

He leaned in to kiss her and she let him. She wanted to believe what he said. She wanted to put stock in the way he spoke about "their" life. What she realized was that when it came to Charlie McMillan, she just plain wanted. She pulled him down on top of her, pushed his jeans from his hips, and wrapped her legs around his waist.

He lifted her nightshirt over her head and latched tightly onto her nipple, sucking and biting as he held her breast firmly in his hand. Her body responded immediately and her panties grew wetter with each tug, but he didn't stop to move lower. He stayed at her breast and worked it harder. Her insides were on fire, wanting and needing to be filled by his cock. She felt him hard against her thigh, but his other hand pinned her arms above her head. She couldn't reach out for him or find her release.

"Fuck me," she growled at him, hearing more anger in her voice than she thought she was feeling.

"No," he responded with a temper of his own.

She pushed her hips against him trying to place the tip of him inside of her, but he evaded her every effort.

"Please," she groaned. "Give me your cock."

"Not yet," He continued sucking her nipple. The biting hurt but with every scrape of his teeth, lightning bolts of pure pleasure shot through to her center. She never thought she could be this close to coming from a man sucking her tits.

"Charlie!" She let the frustration fill her voice. "You have got to fuck me. I need you inside me, please."

"Don't call me Charlie when you're telling me what to do." He stopped sucking to look up at her. "I'm in charge of what's happening here, if you haven't figured that out by now." Cold air assaulted her aching nipple as she shivered. He was breathing heavily, "If you want me to stop, just tell me now. I know we're both emotional, but I don't want to hurt you, Hannah."

He let go of her arms and she rubbed her wrists with her hands.

"You're not hurting me, Charles."

She placed her hands on his shoulders and grabbed his erect dick, centering its head at her core. She raised and lowered her hips, guiding him into her, gasping at the size and weight of him as he filled her.

"Fuck me," she said softer this time, the anger drained from her body.

He responded to her words and her tone by moving forward and up. When he heard her gasp, he retreated and began again. He thrust deeper and harder at each of her moans.

"Touch yourself, Hannah. I want to see you come with me inside of you."

She reached down and ran her finger over her swollen clitoris. Tiny currents of electricity rushed through her, mixing with the deepening ache in her center. She rubbed gently at first, but pressed harder as he increased the speed of his thrusting. A feeling of inevitability overtook her and she felt the trembling start in her toes.

Charles grabbed her ass harder and plunged into her over and over. She closed her eyes and moved her hips against her own fingers and his cock. She heard herself groaning with pleasure as the sensations washed over her. He hardened inside and called out

49

her name as he found his own release.

CHAPTER EIGHT

Hannah did a decent job of pretending Charlie wasn't married, at least for few days, but in the middle of her second week of classes, an opportunity presented itself that she couldn't resist. As she caught the subway back to her home away from home she recognized a head of short, blonde hair in the crowd.

"Melanie!" she called out.

The petite woman turned to look for the voice and when she connected it to Hannah, a broad smile broke across her face. She waved her hand and started making her way through the bodies crammed together in the humid, underground station.

"Hannah," she reached out to embrace her. "Sorry about the sweat! This place is an oven."

"Tell me about it," Hannah replied. "I love the ease of the subway but waiting to actually get on it is a real pain. Especially in this heat."

"Yeah, but it beats car payments, finding parking, the cost of gas..." She counted off on her fingers. "So, we haven't heard from Charles since our double date. Everything going OK?"

Double date. So, Melanie really did understand the situation. She'd probably understood it before Hannah did. As much as Hannah wanted to stay focused on the present and keep pretending that Nadia didn't exist, this was an opportunity for information she couldn't pass up. When would she ever get the chance for an unbiased, objective view of what was happening in her life?

"Really? He hasn't called you? I'm sorry," she said.

"No need to be sorry. I figured you were keeping each other busy."

She winked at her.

"Melanie," she took a chance. "Would you have time to stop off for a drink somewhere? I'd really love to talk about what's happening with someone who knows the whole story."

Melanie looked down and checked the small, classic gold watch that wrapped her wrist. "It's almost six, but I don't have to meet Eric until eight. I guess I could just stay in this dress. You think it'll work for a romantic dinner in little Italy?" She tried to twirl in the short black outfit.

"Watch it," an older man in a suit and tie growled at her as he loosened his tie from the heat.

She fell into Hannah giggling.

"Let's go. There's a place about a block from here that Eric and I love."

She followed Melanie up and out through the maze of people making their way home from work and those heading out for a summer evening of fun. As they left the subway Hannah was surprised to feel such a dramatic difference in temperature. The sweltering above ground heat almost felt like air conditioning, for a second anyway. A few minutes later, they stepped into the actual cool air of a small, shotgun style bar with black and white tiles on the floor and a huge polished oak bar that ran the length of the room.

"There's a booth in the back that's pretty private. I'm assuming you want to talk - talk, right?" She emphasized talk in a way that let Hannah know Melanie understood exactly what this was about.

"Yes," Hannah shook her head and followed.

Melanie stopped off and ordered two draft Stellas. The man behind the bar, who obviously knew her, promised to bring them over and they scooted into the small booth with burgandy seats. Hannah put her laptop and purse to the side.

"Thank you so much for coming with me. I love being with Charlie, but other than my PD classes, he's the only social life I've had."

"And I'm sure the definition of how you've been spending your time isn't exactly social!" She laughed.

Hannah felt the color rise in her cheeks. This woman was the same age a Charlie. Why was she allowing her to make her feel like a teenager caught having sex? She was a grown woman, independent and single, there was no reason she couldn't have as much sex as she liked - with whomever she liked.

"I am so happy you came to town, Hannah. To be honest, I'd almost given up hope that Charles might find a way to get a real life. He's been living for other people so long, I thought maybe he'd forgotten he had his own needs to consider."

"You're talking about Nadia?" she asked.

"Ah...Nadia. Yes, I am."

The bartender brought over their drinks and Hannah took a large sip from the tall glass filled with beer.

"I need to know everything. Charlie's told me some of it, but I think there are things he doesn't really get from his perspective."

"Like what?" Melanie raised a finger and called out to the bartender, "Mike, send over some fries when you get a chance." She looked at Hannah, eyebrows raised, "You good with that?"

"Yeah, fries are always good." She smiled. She liked Melanie a lot. If she ended up in New York, they might really become friends. The thought took her by surprise: If she ended up in New

York. Was she really considering changing her whole life for a man?

"So, he told me about the marriage being one of friendship - not love or sex," she started.

"That's absolutely true, at least from Charlie's perspective," Melanie said.

"See! That's what I mean. He mentioned that Nadia has no idea I'm here because she gets insecure about the thought of him with other women, but I think it's got to be more than just insecurity. How could she not be in love with him?"

"Are you, Hannah? In love with him?"

Hannah almost choked on her beer. How should she answer that? Did she even know?

"It's OK. You can hold off on your answer. Let's talk more about Nadia, because I think you're absolutely right in assuming they have very different ideas of what's going on. You know that she became a citizen a few years ago? They don't have to be married anymore."

"That's what caused our first fight," Hannah replied.

"U-huh, I can see how it would. He told you then?"

"With a little digging. I'm not sure he would have."

"How serious are you about what's happening here, Hannah? I mean, is there really a purpose to us having this conversation or will you leave in a few weeks and never look back? It would be easy enough to do."

"Have you met Charlie? Anyone who thinks leaving him would be easy doesn't have a firm grasp on reality."

"I'll pretend my all consuming love for Eric prohibits me from seeing your point. I'm sure my grasp on reality is intact." She laughed again. "I haven't eaten all day, I need to slow down or I'll be drunk for my dinner."

"I can understand why Nadia wouldn't want to leave him, but she can't expect him to give up a family of his own for her. Why would she want to stay with a man that doesn't love her that way?"

"Simple," Melanie said. "She thinks he will. She knows about you, you know."

"Not that I'm here."

"No, but she knows you're the one person who could take Charles away from her. That's probably why he didn't tell her. Why hurt her if you're not going to stick around?"

"That's what he said. Are you sure you two haven't talked?"

"Positive. But I'm sure that's what he said because I know him, Hannah. He's been our friend for years. I also know that he loves you and if he's going to truly settle down with anyone, he wants it to be you."

Hannah mulled it over. How could she really know if he loved her? He'd been in love with an image of her that he'd carried around for years. He was only now starting to really figure out whom she was. She was in the same boat. He'd been the cute neighbor with the exciting life in New York but how much did she even know about him?

Was he really ready to settle down and start a family? And even if he was, what if she couldn't give it to him? Lots of her friends were still having kids but it wasn't a given that it would happen for everyone. What would he be giving up by attaching himself to an older woman?

"You're worried he doesn't really love you, that he doesn't know you because you haven't really ever been friends," Melanie said.

"That has crossed my mind. I also worry about the age difference."

"Well, that's the most idiotic thing I've ever heard."

"Excuse me?" Hannah asked, somewhat taken aback.

"Age is really just a number. It's your soul that matters. Look at Eric and me. We've got 15 years between us but our souls are in exactly the same place."

"You realize that sounds cheesy as hell, right?" Hannah asked.

Melanie dissolved into a fit of giggles. "Yes, but it's true. I love Eric so much."

Hannah felt the laughter bubbling up inside her. Melanie's exuberance was contagious.

When things settled down, Melanie signaled for the check.

"Listen, Hannah. I think you love him and I know that's scary, but when you meet the person that you know is the one, you have to grab that opportunity in the moment. Forget about Nadia. Use this time to convince him and yourself that you have a future together and when she gets back, it won't matter. He'll choose you."

She reached out and took Melanie's hand, "I think you might be right. I just needed to hear someone tell me to do it."

Melanie got quiet and a more serious look came over her face. "Don't hurt him," she said. "His feelings for you are his homeport in the storm, his true north, if you will. If he loses you now, he's lost the dream of you, too. I'm not sure he could take that, and as much as I like you, I'd hate you forever for it."

Hannah gave her hand a squeeze and stood up.

"Hurting him is the last thing I want to do."

"Good. Now get home to him. I've got a date with a sexy older man."

They parted ways at the door. Hannah decided to splurge on a taxi. She was slightly buzzed and didn't want to get on the wrong train at a transfer. As she hopped into the backseat of the cab, her cell rang.

"So you are alive," a male voice rang out.

"Charlie! Oh God. Sorry, I didn't think you might get worried."

"It's fine. Where are you? Should I get dinner on my own?"

"No, I'm in a taxi. I grabbed a beer with Melanie and just didn't think to call. I'll be home soon. We can make something, or go out if you want."

"Home. Sounds good," his voice was relaxed and happy. "Hannah?"

"Yeah?"

"I'm glad you went out on your own."

"Me, too."

CHAPTER NINE

He was sitting on the couch waiting for her when she walked in. He looked up, smiled, and she melted. Her conversation with Melanie, while not really providing her any new information, had definitely boosted her confidence. What was happening here was real and she had the chance to grab what she wanted and make her life what she knew it could be. Who would have ever guessed that little Charlie McMillan would be her soulmate?

His dark waves, wet from the shower, fell across his forehead casting shadows on those reef blue eyes. He had the smile of an angel but she knew there were wicked thoughts behind it. Her body responded immediately to being within a few feet of him. He rose.

"Ready to go?" he asked.

"I just walked in the door!"

"But I'm starving," he said.

She dropped her bags in the red chair and pulled the ponytail holder from her hair, shaking it free.

"So am I," she said and started unbuttoning her white lace blouse. She slipped the sleeves down her arms and moved to the button at the side of her skirt. She looked up to see his reaction. He sat back down and leaned back against the couch, propping his ankle on his knee and lifting one eyebrow. An invitation to continue? She saw him lick his lip and shift uncomfortably. When she looked again she noticed his tented shorts. She let a seductive smile spread and pushed the skirt down her legs, stepping slowly out of it and closer to the couch.

"Hannah."

She heard him breathe out her name as he ran one hand through his hair.

She took another step in his direction, reached back and unhooked her bra, freeing her breasts. The shock of cold air hardened her nipples and she raised her fingers to touch them, all the while staring straight into his eyes. Desire flooded through her and she felt herself grow wet with wanting. She pushed her panties to the floor and stepped out of them. She could reach out and touch him if she wanted.

"Hi honey, I'm home," she said and closed the distance between them, placing one knee on each side of him without sitting down.

He raised his hands and ran them through her hair. When they reached her shoulders he trailed his fingers along her collarbone, then lower towards her nipples.

She leaned her face close to his, placing her lips right next to his but not moving in for the kiss. Their breath mingled as his fingertips teased her nipples. His tongue reached out and lightly traced the outline of her bottom lip before nipping it with his teeth.

A small sound of pleasure escaped her.

She could feel his hard cock straining against his shorts, so she pressed down, making full contact through the cloth. His hands left her breasts and traveled down her waist as he continued sucking and biting her lower lip. He moved them lower and she put her hands on his, stopping him in his tracks.

She opened her mouth and deepened their kiss, for the first time truly giving into the fact that she had real feelings for this man and that what was happening between them was something she could have for a lifetime if she just had the courage to reach for it.

Instead of trying to continue, his hands went the other way and Hannah felt herself being lifted up an off of his body. He placed her gently beside him and stood up, removing his clothes. Naked and fully turned on, he stood before her and held out a hand.

"Where do you want to go?" she asked.

He just smiled at her and led her towards the red chair. He placed her hands on its back and leaned her over so that she stood with her legs apart, breasts hanging. She felt his hands caress her behind, squeezing and rubbing. She could hear him breathing heavily as he slid a finger inside her. He leaned down and kissed her hip, shoving another finger deeper than before.

He pumped his fingers until she felt like she would scream and only when a sob of need tore from her throat did he pull back and replace his fingers with his shaft between her legs, rubbing it against her wetness and teasing her opening. Reaching for him she guided him inside her and pressed back into him until she could feel him deep against her center.

"Oh my God," she whispered as he started to move slowly in and out.

His hands pulled at her hips and increased his speed. With every thrust she felt herself moving closer and closer to an edge, a cliff she desperately wanted to dive off.

"Faster," she called out.

He obliged.

"Deeper," she exhaled with a moan.

He buried himself inside of her.

"Touch me," she commanded.

He leaned farther over and brought his hand between her legs.

He palmed her and rubbed in time with his thrusts. The angle changed but with his hand between her legs it didn't matter. She felt herself rising, higher and higher, reaching for the love she knew he had to give, for the moment of surrender and release.

"Charles," she screamed his name as her orgasm ripped through her.

His thrusting increased and he moaned as she felt him come inside of her.

"Hannah," he whispered and brought her up to face him. "My Hannah."

And in that moment she knew it was true. She was his Hannah. She didn't want to belong to anyone else. This man was the man she'd been looking for her whole life. She lifted her face and kissed him.

"I love you, Charles."

CHAPTER TEN

The experience of her first Broadway show was not one she was soon to forget. She'd been worried that she'd have nothing to wear but was thrilled to come home from her last class before the weekend and find a gorgeous black sheath in just her size with heels to match.

"I checked the clothes you brought and had Melanie pick something up," Charles told her.

When she'd gone into the bathroom to shower two nights later she found the diamond studs and her knees went weak. Charles had been waiting behind the door in his room and when he heard the box click open he'd slid into the bathroom to see her face.

"What? Why? These are too much!"

But she'd already been in the process of trying them on. No one had ever given her such an extravagant gift and while she didn't know why he believed she deserved them, she was confident his desire to please her was pure. He didn't want anything more from her than for her to be herself.

He reached out and pushed her hair behind her ear to glimpse the sparkle.

"Beautiful and classic, just like you."

Hannah tried to pull him in for a kiss but time had been their enemy.

"Meeting Melanie and Eric in an hour and a half. No time for play."

With that he closed the door.

Later, standing outside the theatre waiting for a cab to take them for a late dinner with their friends, Hannah pondered how three weeks had radically changed her vision of the future. On the plane into LaGuardia she could never have imagined how happy and comfortable she would feel not only in the city, but also with him. She'd never imagined anyone could love her so completely.

She still held a small bit of worry that he may be in love with an idea, a vision of her that didn't match reality, but it was fading quicker than she'd thought possible. The old insecurities Jess had planted in her soul festered and tried to contaminate her growing faith that this man might be "the man" but whenever the fears arose, Charles seemed to be right there, holding her hand or gazing at her with affection.

Suddenly Melanie threw her arms around Hannah's neck and freed her from her introspection. She whispered in her ear, "Eric wants to take me home right this minute. He says I've been a naughty girl and don't deserve dinner or drinks."

"What?" Hannah pushed back to look at her friend. "You shouldn't let him punish you for anything, Mel! He can't keep you from having dinner with friends."

It was the blank look on Melanie's face that let her know she'd misread the situation entirely.

"Oh! Oh, of course." She flashed a smile to show her embarrassment. "Then go. By all means, don't let us keep you."

Melanie hugged her again, "Thanks Han." She turned back and said, "You know Eric loves me and would never hurt me, right?"

"I totally do!" Hannah said while laughing. "I was caught up in my own memories for a moment and misinterpreted what you meant."

"OK, well," she grabbed Eric and pushed him into the next available cab, "It was so good to hang! We'll see you guys soon. What do you have, Hannah? Two more weeks to go?"

Hannah caught the look Charles aimed at Melanie. Not a good subject for the evening. She would need to find a way to distract him. She wasn't ready to make a choice or a decision yet. Two weeks, was that really all that was left?

"Bye guys! See you soon." Charles waved, then turned and took Hannah by the arm. "There's a small restaurant a short walk from here. How comfortable are your heels?"

While she wanted to do whatever it took to take his mind off the time she had left, the heels were brand new and not broken in.

"Umm. No walking, please. New shoes and New York don't seem to mix well."

Another cab pulled up.

"Do you even want dinner since Mel and Eric can't go?"

She couldn't read his voice. She didn't want to upset him or say the wrong thing.

"Whatever you want is fine."

She heard him let out a frustrated sigh as he scooted across the seat to make room for her and she waited for the anger to show. When it didn't and she heard him give the cabbie the apartment address, she realized she'd been holding her breath. He relaxed his head and neck against the seat while turning slightly towards her.

"I wanted to take you someplace special. I wanted Eric and Mel to stay." His voice was quiet. "I don't know. It just feels like nothing's going right tonight."

His blue eyes looked tired and a little sad. She traced his eyebrow with her thumb and let her hand cup his cheek.

"Tonight was beautiful. The show, the company, even right now. It's all exactly what I wanted because it's all with you."

He leaned towards her and placed a gentle kiss to the right of her lips.

"I don't want to lose you, Hannah."

She wanted to answer, "You won't." The words formed and pushed at her throat like a butterfly trying to escape a cocoon, but they were trapped. Trapped by her inability to decide if all of this, these past three weeks, were a real enough reason to change her life. She kissed him harder in response.

The cab pulled up to the apartment and he pulled away from her to pay the fare.

"Charles, did you leave the lights on in the living room?"

While he'd given in on the air conditioning, it wasn't like him to waste energy when they weren't at home. He stepped from the cab and placed himself in front of her, holding her back with his arm.

"No. Give me minute to check things out. Stay here."

"But what if you need help? Two is better than one, hot shot."

"Hannah, just stay here. Please?"

"OK." She pouted just a little. Maybe he'd hit the switch by accident on their way out to the show. It wasn't like a burglar would turn on the lights, right? But then it hit her as he walked through the front door. If someone had turned on the lights, they probably had a key, and the only other person she knew who would have a key was…

"Nadia!" She heard Charles say with surprise. "You scared me to death. What are you doing home?"

A woman's voice answered, "I missed you."

It was just an average voice. Nothing distinctive about it, but it

65

mind as well have been nails across a chalkboard to Hannah. A wave of nausea overtook her and she looked around for a place to be sick. Seconds turned into years and she felt older than ever when Charles returned to her side.

"I know." He pulled her face towards him as if willing her to look him in the eye. "I know this isn't what we were expecting. Remember when we go inside though, that it's not what she was expecting either."

"And whose fault is that?" Hannah said with more venom than she intended. The last thing she wanted to do was meet Nadia when she was coming home from a date with her husband. "I'm sorry." She whispered to him. "I just never imagined this playing out like this! What does she think is going on? Did you tell her anything?"

"She knows someone's been staying here, obviously. I told her I had a guest."

"That's it? You're just going to bring me in there without warning?"

"Hannah!" He grabbed her shoulders. "What do you want me to do? She'll know who you are and what it means the minute she hears your name. All your things are here. You don't have anywhere else to go. And, let's not forget the most important fact, we love each other."

"Do we?" she asked.

His eyes narrowed.

"You're nervous and understandably so, but don't you dare pretend like the past three weeks haven't been the best of our lives. Don't put down our feelings or what we mean to each other because you're scared."He took her hand in his, their fingers intertwined. "Let's go start our new life," he said. "She's waiting."

CHAPTER ELEVEN

As they walked into the apartment, Hannah could hear Nadia complaining about her flights from the kitchen. She looked at Charles and the need to run overcame her.

"I can't do this," she whispered.

He ignored her pulling her forward but shielding her slightly behind his broad shoulders as they stood under the kitchen doorframe.

"Nadia, You remember Hannah, from Ohio."

"Of course," She added stepping forward and stretching out her hand. Dark brown eyes outlined in lashes, the length of which reminded Hannah of a giraffe, looked her up and down.

Hannah had no other choice but to step from her safe hiding spot and take the hand that was definitely wearing a ring. She wondered if Nadia had noticed Charlie's was missing yet.

"Nice to meet you, Nadia. You have a lovely home. I've been enjoying my stay."

Nadia's eyebrows raised as if to say, "I bet you have," although her actual words were, "I'm so glad."

She commented on Hannah's things in what she called the guest room. Hannah assumed she probably thought she'd been sleeping there, too. It dawned on her that this show of being a wife was probably just that, a show. Charles hadn't had time to explain that she already knew their situation, so of course she would play the part.

"You two look very nice. Out for a night on the town?"

"I took Hannah to her first Broadway show. We were supposed to have dinner and drinks with Melanie and Eric, but they bailed."

At the mention of Melanie and Eric a look almost like jealousy passed quickly over her face. "That's too bad."

Hannah tried but she couldn't quite read what was happening. On the one hand Nadia seemed perfectly pleasant, but it was as if each word that came out of her mouth had numerous meanings.

"Well," Hannah said deciding to be brave and just put everything out in the open, "I'm sure you must be really tired from the flights. Let me move my things out of your room. I haven't been sleeping in there anyway."

Charles coughed uncomfortably and squeezed her hand hard. Except for the ever-present sound of sirens and city life, silence filled the room. Nadia blinked a few times, unsure of what to say to the confirmation that this situation she had come home to was indeed more than a friendly visit from an old family friend.

"I am," she said quietly. "Tired that is."

More silence.

"I'll go move my things," Hannah said. She pulled her hand free and turned quickly towards the blue room. With every step she took, her anger and embarrassment grew. If he had just told Nadia the truth from the beginning she wouldn't be in this mortifying situation. If he had been brave enough to risk the safety of his friendly marriage of convenience, maybe things could have been different.

She began throwing things into her bag. Each shirt became a curse word and before she knew it she had strung together a chain of profanity of which she hadn't known she was capable. She looked around the room obviously intended for his "wife" and let the feelings overtake her. Had she been used? Did he even want her to really consider a life with him or was she just a fun time until Nadia returned. Had he expected her to end things and return to Ohio for good? Maybe that's why he hadn't told Nadia she was there. He thought he could satisfy a childhood longing and stay in his charade of a marriage.

The anger led her into the bathroom where she packed up her shampoo and conditioner. Her mind flashed back upon the shower that first day and how he'd heard her calling his name. She flushed in humiliation and reached for her make-up bag and toothbrush. Where else did she have things in the apartment? She needed to get them all now because she was walking out that door and not coming back. Her last two weeks in New York would be on a charge card at the Holiday Inn.

She threw open the door to his bedroom and picked up his T-shirt she'd been sleeping in. She pressed it to her face and the smell of him seeped into every cell in her body. Tears threatened to fall and she dropped it to the floor. She needed to move on. Saying I love you had been a mistake. Thinking this could be real, that she could have a life in the city and with him...just a pipe dream.

She didn't have it in her to hurt or fight with someone like Nadia. The woman was going to stake her claim; it was evident in her eyes. It would get ugly and in the long run she wasn't confident that Charles would actually pick her. Their history may have been chronologically longer but his time with Nadia contained more content.

She heard the click of the door behind her. She bent and picked up the shirt, folded it, and put it on the corner of the bed. Hands framed her shoulders from behind before arms encircled her. His cheek touched her cheek.

"I'm sorry," He whispered. "I know this is hard but please don't leave me."

He turned her to face him, but she looked away focusing her eyes on the dresser and the alarm clock with its red numbers changing before her eyes. Minutes passed before she pushed him away.

"I know you are."

"This can still work, Hannah."

"Don't fool yourself, Charlie. From the moment I arrived, it was all just a lovely fantasy, wish fulfillment on both our parts. Your reality is home now and I'm leaving."

"I don't want you to leave. This isn't some damn adolescent fantasy, Hannah. I love you."

"You love me? You don't show me you love me by inviting me to sleep with you in your bed two doors away from your wife. You don't show me you love me by not explaining from the get go that I am more than a house-guest to her. You want to know how to show me you love me, Charlie?"

He stood staring at her, arms at his side.

"Grow up," she said. "If I've left anything behind give it to Mel. I'll get it from her before I head home."

She returned to Nadia's room and grabbed her bag. She didn't look to see if he was watching, didn't turn to gage the reaction of his wife. It was about her now, not them. She would get a hotel room, finish up these last two weeks of class and go home to Ohio where she belonged. When she got home she would make some changes. She was through sitting around and waiting for her life to happen.

Her dress melted to her skin the minute she hit the hot night air and she mentally berated herself for not taking the time to change out of her heels. She hadn't had time to call a car service so she started the walk to the subway.

"It was fun while it lasted, right?" She whispered to herself. "Two for one off the bucket list…a younger and married man." She took a seat on the subway in between an elderly woman with a grocery bag full of food and a young girl with headphones, eyes closed, dancing in place. Her thoughts immediately flew to their last subway ride together. His hand in her shorts, the things she'd wanted him to do. "God, I'm such a slut," she said to herself.

Reaching down she removed her heels and massaged her arches. She couldn't remember how many blocks the Holiday Inn was from the train. She pulled out her cell. Two missed calls and three new texts. She scrolled through them to make sure she wasn't missing anything important. They were all from him.

She put the phone down before picking it up again. She found Mel's contact info and texted an invitation to lunch the next day. There was no way she could leave NY and go home without hashing this all out with someone and Melanie was the closest thing to a friend she had there.

Her phone vibrated almost immediately. She hadn't expected a response so soon, given the other couple's excuse for not going to dinner.

'On the line with Charles now. What did you do? He's devastated.'

Maybe she was wrong. The closest thing she had to a friend in New York apparently wasn't that close after all.

***

It took a few minutes before Hannah realized the pounding on her hotel room door wasn't part of a dream. She sat up and went to pull her hair into a bun before realizing a few strands were somehow connected to her ear. A quick yank sent a small diamond onto the comforter next to her. Shit, the earrings. She hadn't given them back.

Since the pounding on the door definitely wasn't room service and she knew her card hadn't been rejected there was only one person it could be. Well, at least she could give him back his gift. No need to feel guilty about diamonds. She pushed off the covers and grabbed her robe, tying it tightly enough that no part of her could be considered arousing. This needed to be over quickly, she didn't want to give him the chance to talk her into coming back. She deserved more respect than he'd shown her, more than she'd asked for herself.

She left the latch on the door and stuck her face in the open space. He looked terrible. He had bags under the bags on his eyes. It was obvious he hadn't slept.

"Up all night talking with the wifey?" She baited him. The moment it was out of her mouth she knew she was being childish. She was hurt but that didn't give her an excuse to be cruel. She'd told him to grow up; she needed to display the same maturity she'd hoped for from him. "I'm sorry. That was uncalled for. What do you want, Charles?"

She saw hope in his eyes before he realized she'd used his full name to put distance between them, not out of esteem.

"I want you to come back."

"You can't be serious."

"I am. One hundred and ten percent serious…open the door Hannah. We need to talk."

"No. We don't. I'm not angry anymore, well, I'm almost not angry anymore, but I won't sleep in your bed under the same roof as a woman you're married to when you don't have to be."

"Please let me in?"

He reached out and pushed a strand of her hair behind her ear. "Where's your other earring?"

She stepped back and unlatched the door. He walked in and

she undid the other diamond from her left ear.

"I'm glad you came actually." She held them out and when he didn't move to take them, she pushed the diamonds into his palm before stepping back with folded arms. "I can't keep them."

"I don't want them," he said and placed them on the table by the bed.

"Well, neither do I."

"Fine, leave them for housekeeping then."

"Maybe I will." She lifted her chin.

He took two giant steps towards her and crushed his mouth to hers.

She pushed against his chest. Her insides screamed with desire but her mouth listened to her brain. She bit down on his lip, hard.

"Ow! What the fuck Hannah?" His eyes clouded over and he went to the mirror checking for blood. Rubbing his lip with his hand he turned back to her. "I know I hurt you. I know I should have told Nadia from the beginning. Hell, I know that I shouldn't even be married to Nadia and I promise you," He moved towards her again and she stepped back. "I promise you I won't be for long."

Something inside of her broke open. She'd dealt with too many broken promises from Jess. The desperation in his eyes scared her. She didn't want the extremes or the drama. She suddenly wanted nothing more than for him to leave the room.

"You need to go, Charles."

"Han, didn't you hear me. I'll divorce her. It's over. I let it go on too long anyway. I want you… only you."

She walked to the door and opened it.

"Please leave before I call hotel security."

"I don't understand, Hannah? What happened? How did things

change so fast? You told me you loved me."

"I woke up," she said simply. "You and I, we're pure chemistry. That's all. It would never have lasted. I don't belong here, not too mention the age difference and your marriage." She stepped forward and touched his cheek gently. "The odds were never in our favor, Charles."

He walked towards the door, head hung low. She'd done what she needed to do for them both but she couldn't help feeling like she'd kicked a puppy. She wanted to reach out and hold him, to tell him to get his divorce, that she wanted to stay, not go home, but the old fears overwhelmed her. He may say he wanted to marry her, to have children with her but in the end he would realize sooner rather than later what he was giving up by choosing her and leave. He would hurt her like Jess had, even if for different reasons. She couldn't fail again.

"I will never stop loving you, Hannah."

"Goodbye, Charles," she said as she closed the door, the image of his pained blue eyes burned into her psyche for what she knew would be an eternity.

<u>*PART TWO*</u>

CHAPTER TWELVE

"So Hannah, Tell me more about teaching. How did you end up doing what you do?"

The forty year-old business analyst sat across from her at one of her favorite Vietnamese restaurants. His conversational skills had kept the conversation flowing freely throughout dinner and she had to admit he was extremely handsome with his full head of salt and pepper hair and hipster glasses.

"You know how some people just knew what they wanted to be from when they were little?" She let the question hang in the air and he nodded.

"That wasn't me." She laughed and he joined her. "When I was younger I wanted to be a Vet. I loved animals and my mom wouldn't let us have any so I guess it seemed like a good way to get to be with what I wanted, but couldn't have."

"So, what went wrong? Or, should I ask when did you change your mind?"

"Oh, it was definitely what went wrong. Turns out that I had severe allergies to almost every kind of dog that exists." Hannah laughed again.

Her date didn't.

"Every kind?" he asked.

"Almost!" She shook her head and took a sip of her wine.

"You saw in my profile I have dogs, right?"

The serious tone in his question caught her off guard and she choked a bit.

"I'm sorry, of course I did. It's just a first date though, right? It's not like we have to move in together anytime soon and it's not like you have a wife or anything. It's a dog."

He motioned the waitress for the check.

"Hannah, it has been a lovely evening. You are a brilliant woman with a bright future ahead of you, but I don't like to waste time. If you are as allergic to dogs as you say there's just no way we can be together."

He signed the bill, left the tip and stood.

"I wish you luck in your search. It was so nice to meet you."

Hannah watched as he walked away. He couldn't be serious, could he? This was a joke. Surely, he would turn around and come back, but when the waitress began clearing the table it became clear to her that his dog was as bad as a wife. What the hell had she done in a past life to deserve this kind of crap in her love life?

She slid behind the wheel of her car and pulled out into traffic, hitting the speed dial and speaker on her cell as she did.

"What's up, sis? How was the date with the older man?" Lilly asked.

"He wasn't that much older, and it sucked. I had another date that sucked."

"Hmmm, have you given any thought to the it's not them, it's you theory?"

"Isn't that supposed to be the other way around?" she asked.

"Sweetie, it's been five months since New York. You need to let it go."

"I'll talk to you later, Lilly. I'm driving."

"But…"

She cut her sister off and adjusted the rearview mirror. Let it go. Let it go? The words stung like only a sister's could. It had been five months. Five months of internet dates from hell. She'd put up her profile almost immediately upon returning to Ohio and hadn't had a free weekend since. One thing that the last two weeks in New York without Charlie had taught her was that she hadn't been being fair to herself.

She'd been picking men like Jess and Charlie on purpose, men who couldn't commit, men who were gorgeous and safe, men who couldn't or wouldn't ever be hers. It had been crystal clear to her when she returned that if she wanted the marriage and family she deserved she needed to adjust her settings. She needed a reality check.

It wasn't about chemistry or sparks. It was about practicality. She'd joined an online dating site and checked off every box she thought could possibly lead to a stable, loving, family man and the first box to get marked was between 35 and 50. No more forays into the world of younger men for her.

She pulled into her driveway and grabbed her purse. As she opened the screen door she remembered that she hadn't checked the mail that day. She unloaded the stack of bills, magazines and political postcards and pushed open the front door. The house still smelled like the pumpkin pies she'd made earlier in the day. Thursday was Thanksgiving at Lilly's. "Maybe if I don't talk to her until then I won't be pissed anymore," she muttered under her breath.

She shrugged off her coat and kicked her heels next to the door before plopping on to the sofa to look through the day's mail. Heating bill, water bill, Cosmo, Vote Harry Winfield for Senate! Nothing looked especially exciting or urgent. She went to throw it onto the coffee table when a small white envelope, the type people used to use when they actually wrote letters fell to the floor.

Ms. Hannah Miller was scrawled in black across the front, but there was no address or stamp. She flipped it over quickly scanning for a return address. The flap lay tucked inside, unsealed. This hadn't come by post, this had been hand delivered. Excitement and fear warred in her chest. Did she a secret admirer or a stalker? More likely it was just an invite to a neighborhood girls party where they would expect her to buy something else she didn't need or want.

She pulled open the flap and slid out the white rectangular card. When she did, sparkles fell. "Pretty, but annoying," she said aloud. "Now I'll have to vacuum." Looking at the card more closely she could see it was handwritten but it wasn't a letter or an invitation. It was a poem. Oh shit, she did have a stalker. That's what five months of internet dating got her! She'd tried to be so careful about hiding her personal info but someone must have found her address. She got up quickly to lock the door just in case and then sat back down to read.

If I could be with you
I'd give up the world
Only to give it to you.

If I could be with you
I'd dive to the depths of despair
Only to lift you up.

If I could be with you
I'd feel fear like no one has known
Only to always keep you safe.

If I could be with you
I'd never utter love's language again
Only to do our love justice.

If I could be with you
If I could be with you
If I could be with you...that's the only thing I'd ever do.

    She had to admit the poem was quite pretty, more than that though, it showed that whoever wrote it had listened to her well enough to really know what she wanted. I'll be damned she thought. Maybe there was hope after all. She placed the card on the mantle above her fireplace and walked to the bedroom to change into her pajamas. Stalker or no, she was ready for some sweet dreams and the surprise ode to being with her had been just the inspiration she needed. See world? There's hope, she thought as she drifted off.

CHAPTER THIRTEEN

Thursday arrived and Hannah loaded her pies and cookies into the car to head to Lilly's for their annual family gathering. It had always been her favorite time of year and she loved seeing family members she didn't keep regular contact with, but if she was honest she was slightly worried about seeing the McMillans. Family tradition held that the second half of the evening was open to family friends and neighbors and Hannah knew that Charlie's family hadn't missed a Thanksgiving night at Lilly's in the past five years at least.

"They probably don't even know it happened!" Lilly had tried to comfort her. "As far as we know they have no idea his marriage isn't real in the traditional sense. Why would their son tell them about three weeks of sleeping with you?"

Hannah groaned at Lilly's blunt appraisal of her summer. Was that really all it had been? No, there had been more than sex. It wouldn't have hurt so much if there had been no feelings. She'd since come to the conclusion that what happened between her and Charlie had been very real and unrealistic at the same time.

"You're probably right," she replied. "I just hope they don't have any news to share. I don't want to hear his name, or that he's happy, or heaven forbid that they're going to be grandparents."

"Is that even possible?" Lilly asked. "I thought you said they'd never slept together."

"That's what he told me, but that was five months ago. After I left who knows what went through his head?"

"I do," she said quietly.

"What?" Hannah asked in shock? "How could you know what he was thinking?"

"He called me."

Hannah felt the tips of her ears turn red in anger as the neck of her turtleneck sweater suddenly felt like it was choking her.

"He what?"

"He wanted to talk."

"And you're telling me this five months later?"

"Hannah, come on. You didn't want to know and it wouldn't have made a difference. You started dating again right away and I was hopeful that you'd find someone else soon enough."

"Yeah, we see how well that's turned out."

"Well, you know sis, I was serious about the it's not them, it's you theory. You talk a good game but there's some part of you, an important part, that never left New York."

Hannah knew her sister was right and it made her even angrier. What right did she have to talk with him behind her back? Had she spoken for her? She hadn't told Lilly all of her feelings. What if she'd given him a wrong impression? What if something she'd told him hadn't been true? What if? It suddenly dawned on her that what ifs weren't important if she didn't still have real feelings for him.

"What did he say? What did you tell him?"

"Han, you don't need to hear it, honey. It's water under the bridge. This is what I've been trying to get through your head. It was three weeks, maybe even three weeks of wonderful, but they're over. He's in New York and you're here." She took her hand. "Please, please, please move on. I want you to have a family of your own to bring to these Thanksgivings one day."

"I wanted to move there, you know?"

"To New York?"

"Yeah, I imagined our lives there. Riding the subway with our kids. Going to the museums and baseball games."

"You romanticized it, sweetie." Lilly touched her cheek before moving back to mash more potatoes. "Trust me, married life and a family isn't museum trips and baseball games – even in New York."

"You're probably right, but I think we could have been good together. There was something between us and while it might not have lasted, five months of dating the wrong guys has shown me there was something real to it."

"At least you learned something from the pain." The doorbell rang and she turned holding the bowl in her arms as she stirred. "Can you get that? Joe's out back with the kids playing football. He likes to help but he just gets in the way so he's better off with the children."

"No problem."

She walked to the door trying to imagine the conversation between her sister and Charlie. Why had he called her and more importantly why had she felt the need to keep it from her? She opened the door to the smiling faces of her cousins armed loaded with goodies.

She gave hugs and kisses and relieved them of their offerings before heading back into the kitchen to help Lilly.

"Where's Susie? Isn't she normally here by now?"

"She's at her new boyfriend's family celebration. I can't believe she didn't tell you. Apparently she's convinced he's going to propose."

"Great. That will officially make me the spinster of the family."

"He called her, too, you know."

"What?" Hannah gasped again. "Did he call mom and dad in Phoenix or maybe Great Gram's in Tulsa? Do I need to worry that he rang up my kindergarten teacher or my principal while I'm at it?"

"She's our sister, Han and she is closer to his age than we are. They were always close."

"Uh, at this point I think it's fair to say no one in the family has been as close to him as me."

Lilly opened the oven to check on the turkey. "Crude! But true...and funny. Dinner's ready. Call the kids in from outside and let's get this party started.

***

When the clock struck eight and the McMillans hadn't made an appearance Hannah started to worry. On one hand relief flooded through her because maybe she wouldn't have to hear about his life without her, but on the other she worried that maybe they weren't there because of her. Maybe he'd told them how he felt and they were angry that she'd hurt their son. Just as she was contemplating calling them to make sure they weren't mad the doorbell rang. She heard their familiar voices in the foyer.

"Better late than never," Mr. McMillan called out.

"So happy you made it," Lilly replied.

Mrs. McMillan's gray head of pixie cropped hair popped round the corner, "Has everyone started the games without us?"

Joe stood. "You've only missed charades. We're about to start the new game Lilly picked up in a minute or two. Grab yourselves some beers and get in here!"

For all her sister complained about Joe, Hannah loved his open and friendly personality. He loved people and people loved him. She couldn't have asked for a better brother-in-law. He noticed her watching him and walked over to sit with her. Whispering so the cousins wouldn't hear he said, "Now Hannah, I know you're nervous that they're here, but just remember you're like family to them and I'm sure he never said a word."

Hannah looked Joe in the eye before asking with a calm she didn't feel, "She told you everything?"

He looked hurt. "I'm her husband, Hannah. Of course she did. And she knows I love you and want what's best."

"I am so freaking embarrassed right now."

"No need. I personally disagree with my wife and maybe with you, too. I think the two of you were made for each other, but if you can't see it yet, that's cool. Things have a way of working out." He winked at her and welcomed Charlie's parents into the circle. "Liesel! Chuck! Have a seat. We were just about to go over the rules to this new game."

Before she could say anything he had ushered Charlie's mom into the empty seat beside her. A warm hug enveloped her and she felt tears sting her eyes. When Leisel let go, she sat down and patted her knee. "There, there! I know you've missed us but there's no need for tears."

"Oh, it's not..." she took a deep breath and steadied herself. "It's just the holidays Mrs. McMillan. I get a little emotional this time of year."

"That's one of the things I've always liked about you, dear. You're in touch with your feelings."

When she didn't look away, Hannah wondered if her words were a dig. Surely she wouldn't have hugged her like that if she knew how she'd left her son.

"Your turn Hannah Banana," Mr. McMillan called from across the room. "Draw a card and hum the tune for your team, although it doesn't really matter if you get this one. You don't stand a chance playing with my wife. Love of my life but she couldn't carry a tune to save our son's life."

At the mention of Charlie, Hannah felt the color drain from her face. Card in hand, all eyes were on her as she had to hum the tune and hope for the best. Of course, it was a love song from the fifties and Mrs. McMillen was her saving grace. She sat down happy to be out of the spotlight for a moment.

Leisel leaned towards her as the other team took their turn. "So, Hannah. Any young men in your life these days?"

CHAPTER FOURTEEN

Hannah pulled her coat tighter across her chest as she waited for her defroster to do its duty. Thanksgiving traditionally marked the time of year where there was no returning to just sweaters or jackets and with the frost already on her windshield before midnight, she imagined it was going to be a very chilly weekend. Her thoughts drifted to Charlie in New York. Where had he spent his Thanksgiving? She hadn't had the nerve to ask his parents. Fear of finding out he was with Nadia and they were doing something special or romantic kept her from digging.

Still, she wanted to believe he was happy somewhere. As her thoughts often did when they strayed to him, she began to remember what it felt like to kiss him. She replayed their romantic moments in her mind. The feel of him behind her at the window that very first time she knew they would touch. His hands squeezing her ass as he rode her to a screaming orgasm. She shifted in her seat. If she kept this up she wouldn't need the defroster.

She wanted nothing more than to hear his voice, to have him tell her he wanted her and needed her, to have him say her name as he spilled himself inside her. Damn this age of cell phones. She missed the days when you could call a man, hear his voice and hang up without him knowing who had called.

She started the engine and hit the wiper blades to clear the mush that had formed from the heat blast. Reaching for her phone she contemplated texting him, just to check in or say Happy Thanksgiving. They had always been friends, right? Maybe not real friends until her trip to New York, but friendly enough that she should be allowed a holiday wish for him.

When she reached into her coat pocket for her phone she was surprised to find an envelope, the same size as before with her name written in black on the front. How had it gotten in her coat? Relief flooded through her as she realized her stalker theory had to be wrong. Her coat had been in Lilly and Joe's bedroom all evening, therefore the list of suspects was short. Someone must be playing a practical joke, but the poem in the last card had been so sincere and beautiful. If it was a joke, it wasn't all that funny.

She lifted the flap hoping the glitter accompanying the last note wouldn't make an appearance. Cleaning out her car wouldn't be as easy as her living room floor. She sighed as small gold stars drifted onto her coat and the car seat. It was another poem, but this time short and sweet. "Roses are red, violets are blue, The two most romantic words in the world wait for you."

She flipped the card over looking for the words. A riddle? Whoever was sending her these cards either intended for her to be perplexed or they were hoping she'd figure it out. She reached out and put the car into drive. In a way she was enjoying the attention, she just hoped she wouldn't have to wait much longer to find out who her secret admirer was. Her thoughts roamed back over the past five months of dates. Had she introduced any of them to her family? Who could have been doing the dirty work of putting the cards in place?

There was the firefighter from the next town over that had known Joe in high school. He was a beautiful man to be sure, but she hoped it wasn't him because there hadn't been any physical connection. Her first date back in July had been a friend of Lilly's but he travelled too much for work and they had never found time to see each other again. No, none of the men from her recent dating spree made sense. Besides, none of them knew her the way the writer of the first poem did.

She gave herself a moment of weakness and imagined it could be Charlie. The words, they could so easily have come from his lips, but how? How would he have placed a hand written note in her coat at Thanksgiving, and even if he had come in town for the holidays, the first note had shown up days before. It could have been Susie helping him. Lilly wouldn't have done it but she said he'd talked with Susie, too. Hope swelled in her chest and the ache was sweet and painful.

She pulled into her driveway and walked up to her porch. Her hand stilled at the keyhole when she heard rustling in the bushes to her right. Her shoulders tensed and the bittersweet pain in her chest turned to adrenaline as she place the keys between her fingers to use as a weapon if need be. She slowly turned and saw a chipmunk staring up at her.

"You scared me to death, cutie pie," she said smiling to herself and turned back to the door.

"That was never my intention," a voice from behind her called out.

Waves of nervous energy rolled through her. This couldn't be real. He had to be a dream. There was no way that when she turned around Charles McMillan would be standing in her yard on Thanksgiving evening. She was hallucinating, but she had to know, had to see for herself.

When she turned, there he stood in his black pea coat, collar raised, brown waves tousling gently in the cold breeze. In his hands he held a sign, beautifully designed with stenciled calligraphy. She blinked twice trying to comprehend what it meant.

"Two words," he said.

"I'm divorced," she read out loud.

"Divorced and here for you, Hannah Miller."

He moved towards her purposefully throwing the placard to the porch floor and pulling her into his arms. Warm lips and breath fought against the nip in the air as he lowered his mouth on hers devouring her with a need so visceral it overtook every part of her body. She wanted him in her fingers and toes, in her arms and legs, in her mind, her heart and even more so inside of her. She needed to hold him and feel him moving on top of her, breathing in as he breathed out.

His hands began to unbutton her coat and the chill that reached her abdomen brought her back to reality for a moment. She grabbed his wrists and stopped him.

"No, Hannah. Please don't send me away. I love you. I'm ready for you. I've done what you asked." His eyes stared intently into hers. "I grew up."

She put a finger to his lips.

"It's cold Charles. I just want to open the door and move inside."

His shoulders relaxed and she let go of his wrists.

"You're not sending me away?" he asked.

"I'm not sending you away."

She grabbed his hand and led him into her home, watching him take in his surroundings. "I wasn't expecting company."

He reached for her waist and pulled her to him. "You think I'm inspecting your housekeeping skills?" H,e leaned in and pressed his nose to her neck inhaling deeply. "Hannah, my Hannah. I can't explain how much I've missed your smell, your smile...your body. I've been in a constant state of agitation for five months, wanting and needing you, knowing I couldn't have you yet."

She let her fingers play in the curls at his nape and relished the feel of his tongue sliding in and around her earlobe.

"Let's talk later, Charles. You're divorced. You're here. I don't want to do anything but be with you right now."

He lifted her up, cradling her in strong arms. "Bedroom?" he whispered.

"Through the hall on the left."

He carried her into the small lavender room where she suddenly felt slightly sheepish about her exceedingly girly queen sized bed and trappings. It soon became clear that nothing in the room really mattered, though. Her man was focused on one thing and one thing only, her body. He lifted her sweater over her shoulders and undid the blouse beneath, taking great care with each button. It was agonizingly slow with each brush of a fingertip against her skin turning her on all the more.

When he had her naked from the waist up, he lowered his mouth to her nipple and she felt electricity streak through her like lightning straight to her clit. She let out a moan to show her appreciation and her sucked harder, scraping her with his teeth as he lapped with his tongue.

"Charles?" she whispered.

He stopped to look up at her.

"You're wearing too many clothes."

So he stood and raised his own long sleeved tee over his head revealing the abs that made her knees go weak and her lower abdomen tighten. He undid his jeans and lowered his boxers with them. His cock stood proud and hard and she wondered if she could desire anything more than she did him in that moment.

She reached down and slid her own slacks and panties off, opening her legs for him and motioning him towards her. The feel of his skin on hers was like velvet, soft and warm. She slid against it as he moved over her trailing kisses down her stomach, past her hips and onto her inner thighs.

"Oh, God," she wailed as his lips found her center and his long, callused fingers buried themselves inside her. He worked his lips around and around and pulsed his wrist in time with each stroke of his tongue until she was bucking against him unable to control the sensations coursing through her. She heard herself saying, "Don't stop," over and over again as the vibration of the laughter he held back intensified every movement until her world went black and wave after wave crashed through her, drumming pleasure into her very core.

He raised his head and slid up so that they were eye to eye.

"I love you, Hannah."

"I love you, Charles." Her proclamation a barely audible whisper as she recovered from what was possibly *the* orgasm of her life.

He pulled her on top of him and her hair fell over her shoulders around her face. She went to push it back but he stopped her.

"I just need to look at you," he said.

She could feel his unyielding girth straining against her pussy and she shifted her hips to rub against him, back and forth, she shared the slick wetness he'd made happen. When his tip sat poised at her opening again she lifted forward and then sat back slowly feeling every inch of him slide into her. She saw his eyes darken and close as his hands gripped her hips showing her what he needed, setting the pace for his own release.

He was deep inside of her, touching places she didn't know she needed to be touched. Every stroke took her higher and higher towards a freedom she hadn't even known existed. She watched his face, the way he drew his eyebrows together straining to hold back, to bring her to another peak. His lips called her name as she moved up and down, grinding against him, trying to get impossibly closer, reaching for something they both wanted desperately.

She knew when he couldn't take anymore. His eyes widened and she felt herself being flipped onto her stomach. His hand spread her legs and he took her from behind thrusting hard as his breath on her neck came faster and faster. He snaked his hand round her belly and in between her legs resting most of his weight on top of her. She couldn't move, couldn't do anything but accept his plunging cock and his massaging fingers. He was close. She felt it and suddenly she was shaking and moaning as he increased the speed of his thrust and his hand. Out of nowhere she lost total control. There was no time, no thoughts, she couldn't move but she was coming, so hard she heard herself scream, and then with a groan of pure satisfaction she felt him come into her and collapse at her side.

"Holy shit," he said quietly and he pulled her against him to spoon.

She didn't know if she could speak yet, the experience had overwhelmed her to the verge of tears. Losing total control like that, letting someone into herself completely, she felt like she had made love for the very first time in her life.

"You're mine, Hannah."

"I'm yours, Charles."

She let herself melt into him as she drifted into a heavy sleep.

***

He was staring at her when she woke. If it had been any other man she probably would have been creeped out, but the gentle look of total acceptance and love that lit his face was almost more than she could bear.

"Good morning," she said and nuzzled her face between his shoulder and arm.

"Good morning, gorgeous." He placed a kiss on the top of her head. "We should talk today," he said.

Fear flooded her veins for a quick second before she intentionally relaxed her muscles and gave into what she had learned to call trust. She trusted him. He'd done what she asked. He'd come half way cross the country for her and he shared every bit of himself with her last night. Talking was good, not scary. Talking was the pathway to their future, a future she was now positive that she wanted very badly.

"Yes," she nodded. "Talking is good, but breakfast sounds better. Want me to cook?"

He laughed at that.

"Umm, let me think about it." He rolled his eyes and pretended to be in deep thought. "That's a negative, Ghost Rider."

She laughed. "Look at you throwing movie references older than you are. OK then, does that mean you want to cook?"

He shook his head and suggested they throw on some clothes and eat out somewhere. "I've heard that new breakfast place downtown is pretty good, what's it called again?"

"You mean the Bacon Shack?"

"Definitely. Just the name makes me salivate."

"OK, let me grab a shower though." She started to rise and he pulled her back down.

"I don't want you to shower. Don't you have a baseball cap or something to throw your hair up with?"

"Yeah," she answered and sat up, "but why can't I take a shower first?"

He nuzzled his head against her belly and let his hands massage her ass. "Because you smell like sex and the caveman in me wants you to wear my mark around all day long." He pushed her back against the pillow and kissed her hard.

She let him kiss her for a good full minute before she acquiesced.

"Oh my God, fine. I'll throw on a cap, but you better hope we don't see anyone we know."

His face fell and she backtracked.

"Because I'll look like crap, Charles – not because we'll be together. I promise, I'm all in this time. There's nothing holding me back.

"Let's get going then." He flashed her a boyish smile and threw back the covers to reveal a huge morning hard on. "Nothing you have to do anything about," he teased. "I'm actually more turned on at the thought of bacon right now."

"Asshole," she said, laughing as she left the room to get ready.

CHAPTER FIFTEEN

The hostess at the Bacon Shack informed them that there would be about a thirty minute wait for a table considering it was Black Friday and the early morning shoppers were all looking for a place to rest their feet and refuel for more afternoon festivities. Hannah had totally forgotten there would be crowds everywhere and she seriously regretted allowing Charles to talk her into the baseball cap.

"What if I run into students?" She whined.

"Hannah! You teach third grade. It's not like they'll take one look at you and think you've come from a night of debauchery. They'll think you look tired, or they won't notice at all."

"Their parents will," she huffed.

"I don't think you should be worried about your students or their parents." He sat on an open window ledge that served as a waiting place and pulled her by the hand to sit on his lap. "If anything, I'd be more worried about your sister and her family, as they're eating right over there against the wall."

Hannah looked to her right and gave a horrified gasp as she spotted Lilly, Joe and the kids at a large table towards the back of the restaurant. "Shit, have they seen us yet?" she asked while hiding her face in his chest.

"They have now," he laughed. "Come on, Hannah. They're

family and it's Black Friday. It looks like they're just ordering, and there's space at their table."

She looked at his face full of obnoxious excitement at the prospect of joining her family and smacked his chest.

"You planned this, didn't you?"

"No, I promise," he said as he pinned her wrists together with one hand and kissed the tip of her nose. "But part of me wishes I had. It's worth it to see you turn this particular shade of red."

When she looked back she could see the shocked look on her sister's face and Joe vigorously waving for them to join the party.

"Let's go, sunshine," he said to her. "Time to make us official."

As she walked towards the table where her sister and brother-in-law sat with their three children it reminded her of the walk of shame out of the dorms when she'd stay over with guys in college. She was certain that everyone around her was staring and wondering what that beautiful, young Charles McMillan was doing with old Ms. Miller from the school. She imagined their looks of censure and glares of judgment.

"Happy Black Friday!" Charlie called out to everyone as he shook hands with Joe and gave a quick hug to Lilly. "Getting lots of toys and presents today, kids?"

Lilly made the introductions, "Everyone, this is Charlie. You remember Leisel and Chuck from last night? This is their son who lives in New York. I guess he's home for Thanksgiving," she added, sounding seriously peeved.

"Why weren't you at the house last night, then?" Delia the oldest of the three asked.

"I was there for a second, I just didn't get to talk to anyone but your daddy," Charlie answered.

The icy glare Lilly gave Joe at that revelation was enough to turn the kid's lemonades into slushies. Hannah could tell that Joe hadn't shared that bit of info with his wife. That's why he had been so encouraging and said he thought she and Charlie belonged together. He'd known what was happening all along.

"I think," Joe said loud enough for everyone in the restaurant to hear, "Charlie is more than Leisel and Chuck's son, kids. This is Aunt Hannah's new boyfriend."

"Ooooh," teased Thomas, the middle boy of the family. "Hannie's got a boyfriend. Hannie's got a boyfriend."

At that, she saw Lilly rise from her seat and place her napkin on the table. "I need to get something I left in the car. Hannah, would you come with me?"

"I don't think…" she tried her best to stay at the table.

"Now, Hannah. I really need your help."

She felt a hand take hers and squeeze hard. "We'll be right here waiting. It's cool."

He gave her a wink and she let out the breath she'd been holding. Of course it was cool. She was an adult and she was in love. She was a normal woman having a Black Friday breakfast with her boyfriend, who had happened to run into family. Sure, it was all new and a little awkward, but there was nothing wrong about anything happening between them. She thought back to the sign he had held in her yard the night before.

"He's divorced," she said to Lilly as soon as they walked out the front glass door.

An incredulous look passed over her features, followed by confusion, and then something unexpected – a smile.

"What?" she almost screamed. "Since when? How did that happen? Why does Joe know what's happening and I don't?" She crossed her arms and leaned back against her car.

Hannah shrugged her shoulders "We really should have

grabbed our coats."

"Talk fast then, and make it good," her sister added.

She almost didn't know where to begin but she started with the first note the night of the disastrous date with the dog owner. "I didn't know who it was from, but it was the most beautiful heartfelt poem I'd ever read. I couldn't believe it was about me."

"He wrote you poetry," Lilly sighed.

"I wanted so badly to believe it could be from him, but there was no stamp or return address. I assumed it had to be from someone in town, and then last night in the car I found another note in my pocket with my phone. It was a riddle saying there were two romantic words waiting for me at home."

"That son of a bitch," Lilly said with a smile. "Joe knew all along. He put the note in your coat. That's why no one saw Charlie last night."

She shook her head, "And when I got home he was there in my yard, holding a sign that said, 'I'm divorced'."

"Oh my God, I'm going to die from the sweetness of it all."

"Lilly, do you think it's OK? Do you think I'm doing the right thing? He's younger and he's half a country away…"

"New York isn't half a country from Ohio, Han. Stop being so melodramatic. In my mind the only obstacle you two faced was the fact that he was married, and despite what you told me, I just didn't think he was serious enough or mature enough to do what needed to be done to really be with you. But, he did! He's sitting in there at the table with your family, letting himself be called your boyfriend, and you have obviously spent one hell of a night together. You could have at least showered," she teased.

Back at the table, Charlie glanced her way to make sure things had gone all right. She nodded and sat down. What followed ended up being the most normal and fun family breakfast she'd experienced in ages, maybe ever. The kids loved her new boyfriend and Lilly and Joe showed their support through conversation and laughter. When they rose to give their table to the waiting masses, Hannah felt better than she had years. Things were finally falling into place.

Outside the Bacon Shack, Charlie pulled her into his arms for a kiss that shouldn't have happened in public.

"Wow," she said under her breath. It was all she could manage to say in the moment.

"Should we talk?" he asked.

"I almost hate to say yes. After that kiss, talking is the furthest thing from my mind."

"True," he agreed, "but we can't get to anymore of the good stuff until we get things squared away. I'm not here just to sleep with you, play boyfriend, and head back to New York, Hannah. We're talking life changes here, no small moves."

The words scared her, but the feelings that accompanied them didn't. She knew he was right. When you found love like what they shared, you needed to take risks. He'd taken a huge one for her by leaving Nadia. While his marriage may have been one of convenience, it worked for him. He'd been comfortable.

"You're not talking about leaving New York, are you?"

"It wouldn't be my first choice, no. I have a really good job that I can only see myself moving up in, and if I'm honest, I love the city almost as much as I love you. Almost," he said. "Do you want me to leave New York?"

"No. No, I love the city, too and my teaching certificate is transferrable. I can teach anywhere I go with a little paperwork and a few fees."

He opened the car door and waited for her to get in before closing it behind her and walking to the driver's side. After turning the key in the ignition and adjusting the volume on the radio he asked, "So you're serious then? You could see yourself in New York with me?"

"I am."

He drove in silence, but the smile on his face told her everything she needed to know. "So, that's it then? I'm moving to New York and we're living together?"

"What? No!"

His sudden anger surprised her.

"Why would you ever think I wanted to just live with you? I'm talking the whole deal, Hannah, marriage, kids, and the works. I would never insult you by bringing you to a whole other state with a brand new job and friends without marrying you."

She felt like an elephant suddenly sat on her chest. It was what she wanted, right? It was what she'd waited and waited for Jess to offer, but now that it was being put out there for real she was shaking and sweating profusely.

"Are you OK, Hannah? I know we only talked briefly about this, but I thought it was what you wanted. I know you struggle with feeling like you deserve it, but you do, and I want to give it to you. I want to give you my life and make it ours."

She closed here eyes and took three deep breaths.

"I'm OK," she said. "Just a lot to take in all at once. Yes, you're right. It is what I've wanted, and I did have huge issues with Jess and the fact that he kept putting me off over and over again, but now I think that was because he knew he wasn't the right person for me. I just couldn't bring myself to see it."

"That sounds like you're giving the bastard a lot of credit. You told me he didn't physically abuse you, but the way he treated you didn't sound good."

"I let him, though."

"Bullshit, Hannah. We're starting this relationship out with one hundred percent honesty. None of how he treated you was your fault. You were in a relationship. You had every right to expect respect and forward movement. You were his loss, not the other way around."

She reached for his hand, "Thank you."

"You're welcome."

"You're right. I know I deserve respect and forward motion as you put it. That's why I left you in New York in June."

"Really?" he asked.

She thought she heard hurt in his voice, but what did he expect? He'd been married to someone else. She definitely deserved more than that. " I knew that the feelings I had for you deserved a real chance and they'd never get that if I just accepted the fact that you were with Nadia and let you think everything was OK, but I had no idea what you were going to do, so when I came home and I started looking for what I deserved instead."

"What does that mean? Looking for what you deserved."

He pulled into the driveway and she pulled her feet up under her, took off her seatbelt and faced him. "Exactly what it sounds like. I knew I deserved a husband and a family so I started looking for him. I joined an online dating site and went on easily 25 to 30 first dates."

The muscle in his jaw began to pulse. He had obviously not expected this confession.

"So you mean to tell me that while I was having horrific, agonizing conversations with one of the best friends I've ever had, while I was trying to save her self-esteem and our friendship in a way that would allow me to pursue the future I've wanted with you since I was 10 years-old, you were dating thirty different men? What the hell, Hannah?"

She couldn't suppress the giggle. She tried, but the more she tried the more she laughed, and the more she laughed the angrier he seemed to be getting. That made her laugh harder.

"This isn't funny," he said, but she could see the corner of his mouth start to twitch. He sighed. "How many of them did you kiss?"

"All of them," she squealed. She couldn't help it. He deserved to be messed with.

"What?" he asked, the smile gone again.

She took a few really deep breaths and tried to calm herself down, but the giggles kept coming whenever she looked at his face, which had turned a deep shade of purple.

"OK, OK…hahaha. No, really. Charles, listen to me." She reached out and rubbed his shoulder. They were all first dates. I didn't go on any seconds, and I only kissed 5 or 6 of them. I promise."

He looked at her with slight suspicion.

"You went out on thirty first dates and no one asked you on a second?"

"I didn't say that," she said. "I had quite a few offers that I turned down because I couldn't get a certain man from New York out of my head."

"Really? You really didn't sleep with any of them?"

She raised her shoulders and gave him her most serious look, " I said I didn't even kiss more than five or six. I am not a slut, Charles."

He instantly looked apologetic.

"Let's go inside," he said.

"Let's."

CHAPTER SIXTEEN

She wondered how he would propose. The thought seemed so presumptuous and so wrong that she chided herself in her mind. Best just to let things take their natural course she thought as she cuddled against him in the corner of her sofa watching the fire they had built together. He'd made it clear in the car that he was planning on marrying her and she should trust in that, but then it occurred to her that maybe he considered that a proposal. There was no way in hell she would tell her children one day how daddy had gotten mad at mommy for thinking he just wanted to shack up with her and that's how they got engaged.

"You know," she lifted her chin to look up at him, " You aren't getting away with just telling me we're getting married. You have to ask, and I have to say yes."

Big blue eyes drank in every inch of her face. He was beautiful. How had she gotten so lucky as to be loved by him? And not just loved, he'd confessed to building his future with her in his head since he was ten years-old. She was more than loved; she was wanted.

He didn't answer, just leaned down and kissed her softly on the lips. The mixture of the heat from the fire, the sleepy haze in her brain and the sexy look in his eyes had her deepening the kiss and turning to press her breasts against his chest. His hand moved up to cup her over her sweater. He began massaging her nipple and lowered his mouth to her neck. She let out a long, slow, sigh. As if on cue he lowered his hand and ran it between her legs carefully staying on top of her jeans.

"This is what it would have been like to make out with me in high school," he told her as he continued sucking and licking her neck. "I would have been scared shitless to put my hand under your sweater for fear you'd have made me stop what I was already doing." He continued rubbing between her legs. "Damn it. Is it possible for me to feel how wet you are through your pants?" he asked.

She laid her head back and nodded. She didn't want to do anything to stop the crazy sensations floating through her body. She was butter in his hands and oh, what hands they were.

"What time are your parents supposed to be home?"

She momentarily lost focus on her arousal before realizing he wanted to play a game. Since what he was doing felt like heaven on earth, she decided to go along with whatever he said. She knew that no matter how the game progressed she'd be walking away with a win.

"Not until late, a few more hours at least, but maybe we should move to a room where we're not so out in the open just in case. Would you like to see my room?" she asked in her best teen girl voice.

He groaned and she knew she'd played the part just right. He nodded and she pulled him up by his arms and guided him down the hallway.

"I'm not supposed to let boys in my room, but I'd rather get in trouble for that than have them find us making out on the couch."

"I totally understand," he said and let her lead him down the hall.

"So this is it," Hannah said as she led him into the room he'd made love to her in the previous night. "It's pretty girly, but that's my style. I like being a girl."

"I like you being a girl, too," he said, almost breaking character. "So, this is a really comfortable bed you have here." He pounced on her pillow and put his hands behind his head.

"Yes," she said shyly as she sat on the bed with him, edging closer and closer.

He looked into her eyes and reached up to touch her face. "Hannah?"

"Yes," she held her breath waiting for his request.

"What did you do with all your Rolling Stones posters? I thought they were your favorite?"

She suddenly felt confused. The Rolling Stones were from the seventies. She didn't even know any of their songs. Why would he ask her about posters from an old geezer band? And then she saw the corner of his mouth curve upwards at her bewilderment. He was calling her old. She reached back to smack him playfully, but he caught her wrist in his hand and in one swift move pinned her to the mattress.

"Teen Hannah is enticing, but I like woman Hannah more."

His hand was already down her pants and his fingers danced around her most sensitive spot. She could barely breath, the air thick with her own desire and arousal.

"I want you to come in my hand and then I want come in your mouth. How do you feel about that, Hannah?"

The word yes was already on her lips and rolled easily off her tongue while he added his palm to the work his fingers were doing between her legs. The space between her jeans and her skin was so slight that his hand didn't have room to do much else, but what he was doing was working in a way she'd never expected. When he managed to move his fingers lower and slid one inside she clamped her muscles around him hard and pushed up against him.

"Come for me, Hannah. I want to see you let go. Come for me, baby."

The heat of his palm against her clit and the small movements of his fingers inside her, trapped against her skin, pushed her over the edge and she cried out his name.

For a moment they just laid there together, listening to each other breathe. He was watching her intently when she opened her eyes. "My turn," he said and she smiled. She wanted to give him what he wanted, wanted so badly to make him feel all of the insane things her body was feeling, but she stood first and removed her clothing piece by piece while he watched in fascination.

"If I ever get tired of watching you strip, just go ahead and kill me," he teased.

She kept her eyes on his as she let her bra and panties fall to the floor.

"How wet were those panties?" he asked with a laugh and what she thought sounded like pride in his voice. She didn't answer. She walked slowly over to the bed and began to undress him, pulling him up and throwing his tee to the floor. She pushed him back against the pillow and straddled his knees while she unbuttoned and unzipped his jeans.

"Lift," she said softly, tugging them from his tight ass down to his well defined quads. She rose up and reached behind her pulling them all the way off, and sent them to be one with his shirt. "You, Charles McMillan have been a very good boy, and good boys get rewarded. Is that what you want, Charles? Do you want a reward?"

She saw him swallow hard before nodding. It was nice to see that the effect her words and movements had on him went beyond the hard cock bouncing slightly against his abdomen.

But, that cock was her focus now. He wanted to come in her mouth and she wanted to make him. She lowered her head to his shaft and ran her tongue from the tip to his balls. His groan of approval let her know he wanted more so she added her hand and began stroking as she sucked. Up and down, licking and swirling, she loved the power she felt when he was thrusting into her mouth.

"Slow down, Charles. I'll take you there, I promise, but first..." she reached into the drawer of her bedside table. His lids dropped lower when he saw the silver bullet shaped vibrator she held in her hands.

"Is that for me?" he asked in a hoarse voice.

"Is there a problem if it is?"

He simply shook his head and she lowered hers again. She began to lick and suck while grinding him with one fist. In the other, she flipped the switch to the lowest setting on her silver toy.

His eyes were still closed but he let out a loud moan when she placed it behind his balls, not quite on his ass. She could feel him stiffen and pulse. He wouldn't last much longer so she intensified her tongue movements and switched the toy to medium.

"Holy shit, Hannah!" He cried.

He came in her mouth with a force that almost had her stepping back but she stayed where she was and let his orgasm play itself out.

When his pleasure had subsided and she stretched out beside him he looked her in the eyes, "Marry me," he said.

"Nope. Can't tell the kids about this proposal either. You're zero for two McMillan. Better step up your game."

CHAPTER SEVENTEEN

"So how long are you staying in town," Joe asked Charlie as they all sat around Lilly's kitchen table eating leftover Thanksgiving turkey.

Charlie swallowed a heaping bite of mashed potatoes, "God Lilly, I love these potatoes. Does Hannah know how to make these?"

Lilly stifled her laughter.

When he got no response, he turned to Joe. "I used my two weeks vacation to come home and I was hoping Hannah would return with me over her Christmas break. That way she could start interviewing at some schools. I have a few friends that are teachers. One is a principal at a very cool new charter school and I think we can make something happen."

He smiled at her and her insides turned to mush.

Lilly spoke up, "So Hannah, you're really thinking of moving, huh?"

"I know, I know. It'll be the first time the sisters will be split up, but I have to do what's best for us, and you already know how much I love the city."

"But," Joe interjected, "You'll be home after Christmas right? You wouldn't find a job and leave right away?"

"She'll be home," Charlie said before she could answer. "She has to plan the wedding before I'll let her move."

Silence surrounded the table. Hannah broke it.

"I'm not planning a wedding until Charles actually proposes."

"I guess I missed the getting married part," Lilly jumped in. "I mean, it's great, and I want that for you Han, but don't you think this is all a little fast? Moving to New York, making it legal? Charlie, come on – you just finalized your divorce."

"I know that you know my marriage was never a real marriage. Why would I want to wait to start the life I've already waited years for? One I never thought would happen in my wildest dreams."

Hannah felt his hand on her knee. "She'll get her proposal when she least expects it, and she'll come home to plan our wedding so we can start our lives right.

A sense of warmth settled over her as she listened to him talk with her sister and Joe. He had a plan and she needed to trust in it. This had been the first she's heard about his teacher friends, or spending the holidays with him, but if he could find her a job and wanted her with him she had no reason whatsoever to deny him. More than that, she wanted to go.

"I'll be done with school around the 15th, I guess I can get a flight the day after," she said.

"I've got some extra miles from work that you could use, Hannah." Joe offered.

Charlie started to answer but Hannah spoke before he could say what she knew was about to come out of his mouth. "That would be awesome, Joe. Thank you."

He looked from her to Lilly and Joe, and back again, "Yes, thank you, Joe. That would be really cool."

She stood and put her hands on Charlie's shoulders. "I think it's time we headed out don't you? I know you're off for the next week, but I have school in the morning."

They exchanged a round of hugs before the two of them walked to her car in the cool night air. On the way home she figured it was as good a time as any to bring up what was bothering her. "You know when Joe offered me those airline miles?"

"Yeah, I was about to tell him I already had you a ticket, but you jumped in so quick it didn't seem right so I just said thanks."

"I'm glad you did. I appreciate you picking up on my cue, but what's bugging me about it is that you've already spent hundreds of dollars on a flight for me that you never asked me if I wanted to take. Add to that the job interviews, and assuming I'm spending Christmas with you... I don't know, it seems like a lot of liberties." When he gave her a blank stare she said, "Maybe that's not the right word."

He stayed quiet for a moment. She could tell he was giving his words careful thought, but she kept going because she wasn't quite done with what she had to say.

"I love you, Charles, and I do want to build a life with you. That's not in question here."

He grabbed her hand as he drove. "Then what is it, Han?

"It's just...I don't know. I spent all that time in a relationship with Jess where I had no control over where we were headed. He held all the cards. It was like I couldn't start my future until he said we were ready and he was never going to be ready."

"But I am. So what's the problem? Why is this hard for you?"

She sighed in frustration. "Yes, you're ready, so ready that you seem to have left me out of the planning. It's different from Jess, but it feels the same. You have all of the control here, and even though I'm happy about where we're headed, I want some input, OK?"

"Of course." He looked horrified. "I had no idea that's what it felt like I was doing to you. I'm sorry. I always want you to have a say in every part of our lives."

"But when you talk about our lives Charles, you mostly talk about the life you've envisioned for us. You've had years to know you wanted this with me, but I've only just found you." She looked out the window. She couldn't believe she was going to say this to him but she needed to, so she let it rip.

"If we're going to be together you have to let go of your dreams for us, so we can build our dreams together or we don't have a future." She looked over, astonished to see him wipe the corner of his eye with the back of his hand. "That was harsh. I'm so sorry, Charlie. I didn't mean it to sound so insensitive. I'm being a bitch."

"No, you're not. You're telling the truth. I was so caught up in the excitement of loving you that I haven't given you a chance to love me back. It's really real, isn't it?"

"What?"

"This, all of this." He waved his hand in the air. "I've worried about this moment, about convincing you that we should be together for the past five months, and in every moment since I've come home, I've failed to really hear what you want, past knowing you want me."

She listened to what he was saying. It was understandable. When she left him, he had to start planning, too. She'd started planning for a life without him, but he started planning for how to change his whole life to bring her back.

"Hey," she rubbed his arm and leaned a little closer. "It's OK. This is real, you're right, and it's not going to go away because one of us gets mad or needs to vent. I was being whiny. Not to say that you haven't tried to plan out our entire lives for us. That has to stop, but I didn't mean to threaten what we have together, I promise."

He gave a small smile and was quiet the rest of the way to her house.

"Is it OK if I just drop you off? I haven't been by to see my parents yet, and I know they'll want to know what happened after you found out about the divorce. You've kept me kind of busy since I got into town." He threw her a wink.

"I knew they knew about us." She slapped her thigh. "It was just too strange when your mother asked me if I'd met any nice young men lately!"

He laughed.

"So, they don't have a problem with any of this?"

"Of course they don't. They already considered you family. Hey, you said you have to work tomorrow. Are you cool with me staying the night over there?"

The question caught her off guard. Was he more upset than she realized?

"You'll be back tomorrow night, right?" she asked with hesitation.

"Most definitely." He turned in his seat to kiss her. It was sweet kiss, a soft kiss. "We're OK?" she asked again.

He nodded and she shut the passenger door behind her and watched him drive off.

***

The week and a half that followed Thanksgiving flew by in a haze of rowdy kids ready for Christmas vacation and hours upon hours of fabulous sex. She had to admit that when she put him on the plane back to NYC, her body heaved a sigh of relief. She needed rest and some time to be alone with her thoughts. Charles had been really good about watching his habit of deciding things for the two of them and had made a true effort to seek out her opinion on all kinds of choices regarding their future, the biggest of which was where they would make their home.

When he'd finally broached Nadia about the divorce he hadn't felt right taking her apartment from her, too, so for the time being he was subletting a small one bedroom in Brooklyn. He hoped they could shop around together for a place to call theirs in the week before Christmas. Hannah had been so excited about the possibility she'd immediately gone to Craigslist and started researching places in Manhattan. After she picked her mouth up off the floor, she realized that even with Charlie and her both bringing in decent paychecks Manhattan was a stretch.

Not wanting to admit defeat and tell him her knowledge of how to find housing in NYC wasn't as vast as she'd believed, she decide to just send him a list of her "must haves" and beg off due to school work. Everyone knew the days before Christmas break were like living in crazyville for primary teachers. She e-mailed her list two days before her flight, it included: a guest bedroom, clean bathroom, nice neighbors, a grocery nearby and windows that let in the northern light. His response had been a simple text, "That's it???"

Apparently her boyfriend thought she was easy.

The next day she received another text letting her know that they had four appointments scheduled to see places in Brooklyn and Queens the day after she arrived. "I know you'll want to do the touristy stuff since it's Christmas so we'll get the hard things out of the way in the beginning," he'd said when she called him immediately. Hard things also included interviews. He'd scheduled four of those for her, two on each of the days following the apartment search.

There were moments as the weeks wore on when she wondered what she had gotten herself into. What was the rush?

Did she really want to do everything all at once? But then he would call, or they would fall asleep together on Skype, and she could feel it deep in her heart. This man, this time, this decision was right.

PART THREE

CHAPTER EIGHTEEN

"Hannah! Over here, Hannah!" The familiar voice cried as she searched the baggage carousel for her luggage. Too afraid to look up for fear she would miss her bag again, she held her hand in the air and waved acknowledgement. JFK was an entirely different experience from LaGuardia and she needed to concentrate. Luckily, her luggage made its way to where she waited a fraction of a second before Melanie did or she would have missed it again due to the bear hug. She had to admit that after the way she left New York in June, she never expected this warm of a welcome back.

"Was your flight good?" Mel asked before releasing her. "I saw you went through some weather. Hope there weren't too many bumps. Eeeeehhh! I'm so excited that you're here. True love wins out in the end after all."

She couldn't help but smile at the genuine affection and exuberance the younger woman showed. "A few bumps, yes. This place is crazy. How did you find me so quick?"

"It's not that bad once you get used to it, and I travel a lot for work so I'm here all the time," she said. "Come on, let's go get you a subway card. We're taking the J train into Brooklyn, OK?"

"Lead the way," she replied.

And so it began.

"Get comfortable," Melanie said to her as they found two seats together in the crowd. "It's about 45 minutes to Charles' stop, and then we walk."

They chatted like old friends, catching up after years apart. No one would have guessed they'd only met a total of three times. Hannah was excited to have someone she clicked with so effortlessly to rely on in this new life she was creating. As the train entered Brooklyn she took in the view of the new borough.

"I feel so bad that he gave up his place in Queens. He loved that neighborhood."

"He did," Mel agreed, "but I think it helped assuage some of the guilt he felt over leaving Nadia. By giving her the apartment he felt like he was still taking care of her in a way."

"Do you see her much?" she asked, hoping selfishly that she didn't.

"No, I haven't seen her since before he told her he wanted the divorce. It wasn't like we were besties or anything. Still, I find it a little bit odd that we have so many people in common and it's like she's disappeared from the city."

"Probably on purpose. I can't imagine starting over on my own after losing the man I loved. For Charles it was different, but from what you and he have told me, I feel like she really loved him."

"I don't think there's any doubt there, but we need to quit focusing on her! You're here and you've made your decision, right? You're moving in as soon as you can find a job?"

"I don't know."

Melanie lowered her eyebrows and shot Hannah a look that said, "Don't do this to him again." She looked so intimidating that it made her laugh out loud.

"No! That's not what I meant. Of course, I've decided. I

wouldn't be here if I hadn't. What I meant is that Charles has this caveman idea in his head that I need to go back to Ohio and plan the wedding. He doesn't want me actually moving until we're married."

"Well, we can talk him out of that." Mel stood and grabbed one of Hannah's bags. "Come on, the next stop is ours." As they pushed and shifted to get out of the doors everyone else was trying to enter, she continued, "I get what he's doing. We've talked about this before. He's always been in love with you and he wants it to be perfect. I guess he's already had one marriage that wasn't and he wants this one to be real from the start."

Hannah stopped on the platform to rearrange her coat, scarf and bags. It was crazy how much organization it took to get from one place to the other when traveling. What Melanie said about Charles was so on point. She wondered if she would ever know or understand him that well.

"I guess you're right. It's just frustrating because what I want is to get here as soon as possible, settle in and then plan a wedding together."

"Have you told him that?"

"Not in so many words. We had a conversation a while ago where I let him know I wanted our decisions for the future to be made together from now on, but he'd already proclaimed the stay home and plan the wedding stuff to my family who doesn't want me to leave anyhow." She took a second to look around as they walked under the elevated railways. There were so many people walking everywhere. It was a challenge not to bang into anyone. "Maybe it'll be different here. When we were in Ohio he seemed bossy somehow, almost like he had something to prove."

Melanie raised an eyebrow, "Didn't he?"

"What do you mean?"

"Oh, come on, Hannah. You really can't figure out why he

wouldn't be the same guy in Ohio that he is here in New York?"

She shook her head, "I really can't."

"In Ohio he feels like the kid next door. Your family, his family, he's constantly around people he's had to hide his attraction from since he was young. Not to mention that the things that give him his confidence and independence are here in this city. This is where he became a man; this is where you finally saw him as a man."

"Are you sure you're in real estate and not psychiatry?" Hannah laughed. "That actually makes a lot of sense."

"Thank you," she said as she took a bow, then wiggled her eyebrows. "I thought you liked how on top of things he was when you were last here."

Hannah blushed as she gave that some thought. She had been attracted to the way he took control and led her around the city. When he'd first ordered for her that night in the village she'd been slightly put off, but it was his assertiveness that had allowed her to see him as more than the kid she'd watched grow up.

Melanie stopped in front of a five story red brick building and pulled out a key. They stepped into a hallway that reminded her of something from the 1920's or 30's. Small black and white squares tiled the floors, while intricate moldings climbed the walls. She looked for an elevator but the wide staircase to the right appeared to be the way up. The only thing that marred the retro beauty was that it seemed to be crumbling.

"I know," Melanie said, observing Hannah's glances. "Such a shame. It's gorgeous but the owner just doesn't have the money to make the repairs, plus the neighborhood isn't the wealthiest. You'll find lots of people who can barely afford their rent, but at least it's stabilized in this one and won't keep going up." She paused and took a breath, "Speaking of going up," she pointed to the stairs. "Fourth floor, my dear."

"No elevator?"

Melanie laughed.

Hannah trudged up the stairs, her exhaustion from the traveling starting to overwhelm her. When they opened the door to Charles' sublet she let out a sigh of relief. It was clean and simply decorated with lots of light and a big comfortable sofa that called out her name. She dropped her bags in the entryway and sprawled across it.

"Oh, don't I wish I could do that, too. Unfortunately I have a showing this afternoon. Don't get up. I'll leave the keys on the table," she said as Hannah began to push herself from the sofa. "You're obviously tired and I'm going to see you tomorrow for appointments anyway."

"Thank you so much!" She mumbled and watched her exit before she stood, grabbed her bag and headed to the bathroom. Once inside she pulled out the red satin lingerie she'd brought specifically to surprise Charles. She was definitely exhausted, but there was no reason she couldn't fall asleep in his bed and give him a pleasant surprise when he came home from work. She could think of no better way to begin their official together time in New York.

***

She awoke thinking an earthquake had hit, when in reality Charles had just jumped on the bed numerous times trying to wake her. Her mascara made opening her eyes a slow and sticky process, but once unfastened, they locked on his.

"I can't tell you what coming home and finding you in my bed feels like," he murmured before lowering his lips to hers.

"And I can't tell you what waking up to the love of your life jostling you like he's trying to wake the dead feels like," she answered.

"Surely, you're not upset that I woke you. That red lingerie led me to believe you wanted me to wake you up."

She shifted beneath him, pushing the covers away and wrapping her legs round his waist. He looked amazing. She laced her fingers behind his neck, "Oh, I wanted you to wake me up all right, but I was thinking of a grown man's kiss, not a five year-old jumping on the bed." She pushed up and touched her lips to his.

He shifted back and rested his head on his hand.

"Actually, as much as I love the effort. I've had a really long day. Are you cool if we just lie here and talk awhile?"

She snuggled against his chest.

"Absolutely."

She breathed in the comforting familiar smell of him and kept her eyes closed, reveling in the feel of his fingers in her hair.

"How was the flight?" he asked.

"Bumpy."

"And did Mel give you the tour of our neighborhood along the way? I know it's not the same as before, but it's just for a little while. We'll find our own place soon."

"I love it here. The light is good and it's clean and simple...oh, and the building itself? It's so old and beautiful!"

"And falling apart," he added.

She sighed, "And falling apart. We'll find something tomorrow with Mel. No worries."

"All of my worries disappeared the minute I saw you here."

CHAPTER NINETEEN

"Well, you have a very impressive resume, Ms. Miller. I admit that having attended Columbia myself, I know what kind of continuing education you've received. It speaks to your dedication that you would seek to further yourself at your own expense."

Hannah smiled at the young principal. Jonathan Leonard must have been somewhere in between her age and Charles', but she couldn't quite place where. His clothing choices and warm manner told her that he would expect professionalism and respect, but still offer collegiality.

"Do you have any questions for us?" he asked.

"Actually, I was wondering if you could tell me a little more about the students you serve here. I'm coming from a fairly racially and economically homogenous environment and I'm really looking for some diversity in my life."

He laughed and shook his head. "Well, we can certainly offer you that. One of the things I love about leading Westview Charter is there is only one word that you could choose that would describe all of our kids. Driven."

Driven could mean so many different things. She wasn't sure she wanted to jump into a situation where she would be hounded by parents and so focused on success that she couldn't form relationships. She waited for him to continue.

"Our students are driven to become their best selves, Hannah. For some of them that means they will be the first in their family to graduate high school, while for others they want to continue the family tradition of an Ivy League education. Some are driven in the arts and music, while others excel in the sciences. Our goal is to help these kids find what they're good at and become their best because they love the learning – not the accolades."

He stood and she followed suit.

"It's been a pleasure to interview you. I'm so happy Charles was able to get something scheduled while you were in town."

"Me, too," she said, realizing she genuinely meant it. Her initial anger at his planning their life without her input had subsided.

He walked her to the school entrance and politely inquired about her ability to negotiate the subway back to Brooklyn. As she was halfway down the steps, he called to her, "Hannah! One more question."

She slowly made her way back up. All the walking that New York required seemed to be wearing her out this trip more than last.

"I know Charles mentioned that you would be available next school year and I do have an opening, but is there any chance you'll be coming to the city sooner? I have a third grade teacher taking maternity leave in two months and my plans for her substitute just fell through."

Her head felt heavy and she could hear her blood coursing through her veins. Nervous excitement flooded her body. He wanted her. He was offering her a job for this semester, as well as next year. She had never felt more at home in a school than she had while walking the halls of Westview Charter, but Charles had been pretty adamant that he wanted to do things the right way, and after talking to Melanie she finally was starting to understand why.

That meant her returning to Ohio and planning their wedding before moving to the city.

"I'd have to talk it over with Charles," she said. "There might be a way. When would you need to know?"

"I'm kind of in a bind," he replied. "I have to find someone soon, so I'll be putting the ad out tomorrow. I'd say if you knew by the end of the week we could work something out."

"I'll definitely get back to you one way or another. Promise!"

She waved and headed back down the stairs towards the subway. She thought she knew what Charles would have to say on the matter, but she had to bring it up. It wasn't like they couldn't replace her at the school she was at now. There was a waiting list a mile long of qualified teachers that wanted her job, and being back in the city, back in Charles' arms at night, had only made the thought of returning to Ohio without him more unbearable.

Lost in thought as she boarded the 4 train, she didn't notice until it was too late that she'd dropped a glove along the way.

"Damn it," she said a little louder than she'd meant, and sat down in an empty bucket seat.

A voice spoke from behind her. "Rough day?"

Turning to see who had broken the unspoken rule of not speaking to others on the subway, she looked straight into Nadia's dark, brown eyes. In one quick sweep, she took in the long black ponytail and bulky coat. She carried a bag of groceries on her lap and smiled broadly.

"I lost a glove," she managed to squeak. She felt herself turn fifty shades of red. Running into her like this was awkward as hell. In a city of 8 million people, what were the odds of seeing the ex-wife of her fiancé on a train?

"I've had a rough day, too," she said. "Seems like a rough year, actually. I lost a husband."

Hannah swallowed hard. This wasn't how she wanted things to go. She was just about to say how sorry she was for everything that happened when Nadia doubled over in laughter.

"What?" Hannah asked.

"I just couldn't help it." Nadia continued to giggle. "Your face. I'm so sorry, Hannah. Really. I was just pulling your leg. I don't hold any hard feelings for you anymore. I'm over it. OK?"

There was a pleading look behind the smiling eyes. She seemed sincere.

"Over it?" Hannah asked. "How could you be over it? You loved him. You imagined a life with him. You actually started building one, and then I came and tore it all to shreds. That was never my intention, Nadia. I never meant to ruin your life."

The dark eyes seemed to warm even further.

"You didn't ruin my life, Hannah." There was a pause and Hannah noticed the woman who had been quietly reading across from them now couldn't seem to look away. "If anything you gave me my life."

She shook her head in disbelief. "How?"

A voice echoed through the car announcing the next stop.

"I have to go," Nadia said. "Don't feel guilty, Hannah. It's worked out for the best for the both of us. Really."

Nadia pushed herself up from the seat and scooted past the curious woman with the book. As she turned to say goodbye, her coat fell open. With a quick movement she pulled it closed, but not before Hannah noticed her hand absently caress her extended belly.

"Maybe we can talk soon?" Nadia asked.

Hannah simply nodded as she fought the urge to get sick.

***

"Pregnant?" Melanie screamed.

"No doubt," Hannah confirmed, "and by the looks of it I'd say about five months." She put her face in her hands and groaned. "I hate to say it, but my mind went there. I know, without a doubt that it isn't his baby. I trust him completely where Nadia is concerned, but the timing and the shock of it all? My first thought was that it was his."

"I can't blame you for that."

Doubt started creeping back in. If Melanie thought she should be worried, maybe she should be. She shook her head, stood and began to pace back and forth.

"No, if it was his baby, she would have said something. She loves him. She would never have intentionally not told him about the one thing that would have guilted him into staying with her for good."

"You're right. She knew he was leaving her for you. If she were going to play a pregnancy card, she would have done it then. Maybe she's met someone else. I told you I haven't seen or heard from her, and you said she seemed happy. Maybe she's just moved on with her life." Melanie stretched out on the couch and took a sip of her wine.

Hannah grabbed the glass from Mel's hand and gulped.

"Sure, take the rest of that. Didn't need it as much as you anyway."

"It's just that, when I think back to that time, I'd made it so clear to him I was leaving. I thought it was over. I went on dates. Could I blame him if he had decided to sleep with her? What if I drove him to it?"

"OK. That's enough," she stood and took the glass from her hand. "When you start blaming yourself for the imaginary actions of a man who absolutely 100% loves you, and only you, you're cut off."

Mel walked the glass to the kitchen, came out and grabbed her purse.

"I've got to run. What are you going to do when Charles get home? You going to tell him or not?"

Hannah pulled this pillow against her chest and let out the breath she'd been holding. "I don't know."

"Well, let me know before I pick you two up to apartment shop tomorrow, OK? I don't want to say the wrong thing."

"I will. Do you want me to walk you out?"

Mel leaned down for a quick hug.

"Stay on your couch, you lazy bum. I'll see you tomorrow."

The click of the door was like a trigger for her tears. They started slowly, one by one, before turning into a raging stream that left her emotionally and physically drained. She needn't have worried about what to say to Charlie because she slept through his coming home and woke up to a note on her pillow that he'd meet her and Mel at their Mexican place in the Village for lunch.

CHAPTER TWENTY

"So, I know none of the places we've seen so far have been your dream space, but I have a feeling that the property we're visiting today is going to be the one."

"I hope so," Charles said as he squeezed Hannah's hand from across the table.

It was nice to be out with him. The past few days had been filled with interviews and what seemed like a million details. To top that off, whenever they had down time, all she wanted was to curl up on the couch exhausted from the constant go-go-go of city life. "What is it about this one that you think we'll like so much, Mel?"

Melanie picked up the check and gave them a mysterious smile. "You'll have to wait and see! Come on, let's go get the train."

The wind whipped through her hair as they tread the narrow village streets under grey skies that threatened snow, but Hannah loved the feel of the city this close to the holidays. Everywhere she looked people were rushing around with packages. Storefronts sported lavish, decorative displays that were almost worth freezing to death to admire. She breathed a sigh of relief when they took the escalator down to the subway and her skin stopped burning from the cold.

Charles kept looking at her expectantly.

"What? What do you think I'm going to figure out? I don't have any idea where we're going."

"I'm disappointed, Hannah," he teased. "I would have thought you had the subway system memorized by now."

"Well, I don't, but I can tell we aren't headed Uptown."

A laugh escaped Mel. "Manhattan! As if…"

Charles led them to two open seats and stood while they sat. With each passing stop Hannah started to get more excited. The familiar names brought back memories of her first trip. Could it be that they were headed to Queens?

"Mel, are we going where I think we are?"

She just smiled and looked out the window.

"Charles? Tell me, now!"

"OK! Yes, we're in Queens and the place we're seeing is actually only about a five minute walk from my old neighborhood." He reached out and ran a finger down her cheek. "I'm excited, too. That part of town just feels like home."

When they exited the station she did, indeed, know where they were. She was beginning to believe that if this apartment had just one of her must haves on the list it would be enough. She needed the feeling of belonging this neighborhood gave her. Taking a left instead of the right that would have led them to their old apartment, they walked the three blocks to a quaint duplex that looked as if it had built in the 1940's.

"We'll take it," she exclaimed.

Mel started laughing again.

"How about we go inside first? What do you say, Charles?"

He looked from Mel to Hannah and back again. A broad smile spread from ear to ear and his blue eyes danced with excitement.

"I think Hannah has great instincts. We'll take it," he agreed.

"Jeez, you two! I know we say real estate is all about location, but shouldn't you look inside first?"

"Why?" he asked. "This is where Hannah and I are going to start a family. I can feel it in my bones."

At the mention of family, Mel shot Hannah a look. She'd forgotten about seeing Nadia. She cringed inwardly and hoped she'd have the good sense not to bring it up. Unfortunately, she didn't.

"Speaking of families, are you sure you guys want to be so close to Nadia and the new baby? It could lead to some uncomfortable run-ins down the road."

Charles' face went from confused to ashen.

"Baby? What are you talking about?" He looked to Hannah and she quickly looked away. "Nadia's pregnant? When did you see her? How do you know?"

Mel walked up and opened the front door of the duplex. Stepping back she said, "Why don't I give you two a chance to check out the apartment, and maybe talk a minute." The look she gave Hannah expressed sorrow, but it was small comfort that the revelation had been an accident.

His reaction hadn't filled her with hope. He seemed genuinely surprised and overly worried. The way his face had turned white? Could he be the father?

They stepped through the entry into an open concept living room and kitchen flooded with light. While the outside showed its age, the inside had obviously been refurbished, but looking at the floor, trying to avoid Charles' probing gaze, she noticed beautiful parquet inlays in the hardwood that had to have been original.

"These floors are amazing," she commented quietly.

"How could you have known she was pregnant and not told

me?"

Hannah wrapped her arms around her chest and walked towards the stairway that led to the bedrooms. Taking a step up, she paused and turned.

"I didn't know how. I didn't know if maybe, you already knew."

Understanding broke.

"You thought it could be mine?"

She rushed to his side and took his arm.

"Only for a moment. I was caught off guard. We were on the subway, and she was being so kind. She said she hoped we could talk sometime soon and when she got up to leave her coat fell open and it was obvious. I'd say 5 or 6 months obvious. With the timing and how I left you, I just thought…what if?"

He shook her hand from his arm and walked up the stairs without saying a word. She stood in the open space, frozen, not knowing whether to follow or give him a moment. He hadn't denied the possibility outright, but his pain at the idea she could have thought the child was his was enough to prove to her it wasn't.

"Charles?" She called up the steps. When he didn't answer she turned and walked back outside to Mel.

"What happened?"

"It's not his. He's hurt that I even entertained the idea. I'd also say he's worried about her and doesn't know if he should contact her or offer help, but he hasn't actually said that part out loud."

Mel looked through the doorway.

"He's upstairs," Hannah said. "Let's give him some space."

* * *

The ride back to Brooklyn, with only her looping fears and insecurities playing in her mind, was probably the longest ride of her life. While they had decided on the duplex in Queens and had a move in date for right after the new year, the elephant in the room that neither of them wanted to discuss had tempered the excitement they should have been feeling.

Upon entering the apartment he turned to her. "How could you have even believed for one moment that I could have gotten her pregnant. You knew that we weren't involved physically. Do you have no faith in me?" He sat and pulled his fingers through the waves above his ears in frustration. "I just don't get it."

She sat next to him and grabbed his hand. Opening his palm she laced her fingers through his. "I hurt you."

"Yes, you did." He answered.

"No – I mean I hurt you when I left. When I threw you out of the hotel room and tried to give you back the diamonds. I hurt you when I went back to Ohio and began dating with the intention of forgetting you. I know you talked to Lilly, and Susie, and I know they weren't encouraging." She nudged his chin so that they were face-to-face. "Knowing the pain I caused you, I wondered. Just for a second, but I wondered if maybe I had caused you to turn to her in comfort. If I had, then I would be the one that had caused this whole situation, and I would also be the one keeping you from a life with your child."

"But I didn't. It's not my baby."

"I know that. I knew that. It was one moment of doubt. You know me. You know my insecurities. You know that I have always wondered why you would want me - why you are with me."

He stood and walked to the window. It had started to snow.

"Still?"

"Yes, still Charles. It's not a constant worry, and I've come to believe in us and that you love me and want a life with me, but every once in awhile I can't help it. There are realities to our situation that are never going to go away."

He turned, arms crossed and expression dark.

"I don't want to say anything to validate this insecurity that you feel, Hannah, but I'm angry and I'm not sure how to get over it because it all stems from something I can't control. I can't make you feel my love if you don't. You have to open yourself to it. You have to give yourself to us, all of yourself, even the part of you that's scared to death."

She walked to him and circled her arms around his waist. Pressing her nose against his back she inhaled the calming, manly scent that was his alone. She closed her eyes and held him. "I want to give you all of me, Charles," she whispered.

He turned and pulled her closer.

"I know." He kissed the top of her head before pulling her hand and leading her to the bedroom. Once there he leaned down and pressed his lips to her neck. Trailing soft kisses across her collarbone, he unbuttoned her shirt and let it slide to the floor. He stood back, drinking in the sight of her. She felt the self-consciousness of being totally vulnerable to him, but she opened to it and gave into the fear.

He reached out and undid the clasp that held her bra in place, gently tugging it off and then reaching to cup her breasts. His thumbs circled and kneaded at her nipples. They stood together, never once breaking eye contact, lips hovering but not consummating the kiss that would send them both on this journey into deeper intimacy.

She took his hands from her chest to remove his shirt and moved closer so that her hardened peaks tickled at him with each rise and fall of her breath. He lifted her chin so that their lips finally touched, so soft and quietly that she almost felt pain from the need and tenderness warring inside her.

"I love you," she exhaled.

He took a deep breath in, as if to accept her apology and declaration.

"I love you," he replied.

He lowered his hands to unbutton her jeans and pushed them from her hips while she struggled to free him of his khakis. They stood naked with each other, souls bared, insecurities, flaws and all. She knew in that moment she wouldn't be going back to Ohio. No matter what he wanted or how much he argued. She was here to stay. He was her home.

CHAPTER TWENTY-ONE

Christmas morning dawned with bright sunshine and snow covered streets. She snuggled closer to Charles, reveling in the warmth that radiated from his body. The apartment was in chaos around them, half packed for the move to Queens and half filled with the Christmas decorations Hannah had refused to go without. The tree they had brought up the four flights of stairs sparkled in the corner, a reminder of what they could accomplish when they worked together.

The deep sigh that escaped his lips signaled he was waking up and she took a moment to let her eyes trail over his sleep softened features. He truly was the most beautiful man she had ever seen and despite his lack of officially asking, he was most definitely her future husband. She tried to let go of the excitement that flooded her stomach when she thought of the proposal. She was almost positive it would come today, but she didn't want to be too disappointed if she was wrong.

"Good morning," Charles said in his deep sleepy voice that seemed to always awaken the sexual goddess inside of her. He turned and put his head on her bare chest. "Merry Christmas."

She giggled at the smile on his face and the look in his eyes as he opened them level with her nipples.

"Merry Christmas," she repeated.

"Present time?" he asked.

"You're as bad as a child," she chided.

"OK, then, food first. You wore me out last night. I feel like I could eat a horse. What kind of Christmas morning feast do you have planned for us?" He wiggled his eyebrows up and down in expectation.

"Oh, no." She pushed him off of her. "It's not like I was suddenly blessed with culinary skills in a Christmas miracle. If you want anything other than pumpkin pies or cookies, I'd suggest you go put something in the oven. Pour us some orange juice and champagne, too. A mimosa sounds like a perfect Christmas morning tradition to start!"

He flicked back the covers and stood, stretching like a cat, while the sunlight played on his gloriously naked physique.

"Stop showing off and make us some food," she growled before throwing a pillow in his direction. "Just because I want to eat before presents, doesn't mean I want to wait all day to see what's in that big box under the tree."

"Aha! I knew you were human!" He said as he left the room.

Hannah rose slowly and picked up the pink silk robe from the floor beside the bed. She slid her arms in and made her way to the bathroom to throw some cold water on her face and freshen up. Once satisfied she'd look decent in any holiday selfies he felt inclined to take, she walked to the kitchen. Charles had just slid the cinnamon buns into the oven and was working on popping the cork on the champagne.

"I meant to ask you last night but forgot," he said. "Did you ever hear back from Jonathan about the job for next year?"

She smiled. Time to let him in on her secret. He couldn't get mad on Christmas morning. It would be sacrilegious.

"I did! I got it."

"That's awesome!" He handed her a mimosa and raised his glass in a toast. "Here's to everything falling into place," he offered.

"And here's to shucking the plan and playing it all by ear," she added.

He choked a bit before covering his eyes with his palm, but there was still a smile on his face.

"What have you done now, Hannah?"

"Well, you know that these past two weeks have shown me that this is right – that we're right…"

"I hope so. We're getting married."

"Well, maybe we are. You still haven't asked me, but that's not what I'm getting at. The idea of returning to Ohio and living without you for months before we can start our life here, well, I'm just not OK with that."

The smile on his face lessened. "What did you do, Hannah?"

"You have to promise you won't get mad. It's Christmas and remember we said we were going to plan our life together from now on – not just follow what you imagined it would be like."

He nodded. "I remember. Together was the key word in that statement. Why do I get the feeling you made a decision for both of us?"

"Promise first. You're not going to ruin our first Christmas together over this."

He pulled her into his arms and kissed her hard. "Just tell me before I make something up in my head that's far worse than reality."

She bounced in his arms unable to contain her excitement. "I'm not going back to Ohio. Jonathan offered me a maternity sub position for February through April, and a job for next year. I'm going to be teaching at Westview."

Hannah wasn't sure what his lack of expression meant, but she thought it was a positive that he wasn't overtly angry. "Mel and I spent a long time talking and I know that you wanted me to go back and plan the wedding because you want this marriage to start out the right way, but don't you see Charlie – it's right already. We don't have to follow a script to make things work or to make this real. It is, and we are, and I don't want to wait. I want to be here with you and move into our home and start my job and just...just spend every moment together instead of miles apart."

He took a sip of his mimosa.

"So, what do you think?" she asked.

"I think that we should open our presents now."

"But what about what I told you? You're not angry? We're OK?

He picked her glass from her hand and set it on the table next to his. He still wasn't smiling, but he wasn't visibly upset. "Let's go," he said while guiding her into the living room.

"You're making me nervous. Could you smile at least?"

"Even if I genuinely smiled right now, Hannah, your insecurities wouldn't let you believe it was real. Let's just open our gifts and celebrate our first Christmas together." He sat on the floor by the tree and patted the space next to him. "You first." He pushed the large box towards her.

"I've been wondering what's in this box for the past three days! What in the world did you get me that could take up this much space?"

She saw it then, the slight tug at the corner of his mouth. He was playing her and doing a fabulous job of it. She'd really believed he was angry, but it was all a show. What was he up to? She pulled the wrapping from the large box and was immediately confronted with a smaller wrapped box inside.

"You didn't." She blew out a breath in playful frustration.

He laughed for the first time since he'd brought up her new job.

"You did," she said as the new gift gave way to an even smaller wrapped version until she was down to a box the size of what could only realistically be a picture frame. She hid her slight disappointment at the fact it wasn't the size of a ring box.

"Open it," he prodded.

When she pulled off the top to the small white box she discovered that it was, in fact, a picture frame. Silver and engraved with a photo of the two of them in Ohio, the date on the frame read Nov. 28, Thanksgiving Day. It was the day he'd shown up at her house with the news of his divorce, the day their life together had finally begun.

Tears sprang to her eyes.

"It's so thoughtful, Charles. I love it."

"Really? You're not sad it's not a ring?"

"Well," she shrugged her shoulders, "maybe just a little bit."

"There's another present for you under the tree, Hannah."

When she looked she noticed a smaller box off to the side, slightly bigger than a ring box but still, it was a possibility. She felt her face grow warmer. How embarrassing that he knew how much she wanted this proposal and was toying with her.

"Open it," he said.

She lifted the gold and red wrapping paper, exposing a regular cardboard gift box. She would never admit to secretly hoping for Tiffany blue. She held it up and shook. Whatever it was, it was small and hard. She lifted the top and pulled out a $100 gift card to an office supply store. A post it note stuck to the back of the card read, 'For February supplies…Congratulations, Love'.

She looked up. He was stifling his laughter the best he could. Hannah smacked at his shoulder with the gift card.

"You knew! How did you find out? You let me worry that you would be angry and that I could make a mess of our first Christmas morning when you knew about my job the whole time!"

"Jonathan called me before he called you. He just wanted to make sure things were solid with us before he took a chance and offered you the maternity sub. He didn't have time to fix a mistake if you decided not to stay."

She let her shoulders relax in relief and gave him a small smile.

"So, you're really OK with me staying."

"I'm really OK with it, Han. Promise. In fact, you were right and I was wrong. I want you to stay. I don't want to wait another minute to start our life together. He pushed up to his knees and reached up onto the tree where a small clear glass ornament hung. Funny, she didn't remember hanging that one.

He held the ornament in his open palm and leaned closer for her to see. Something glinted in the sunlight and she suddenly couldn't catch her breath.

"Hannah Miller, love of my entire life…will you be mine?"

Inside the glass ornament, an elegant emerald cut diamond set in white gold waited for her finger. It was the most beautiful ring she'd ever seen.

"What? How? How did you get it inside? More importantly," she was nearly screaming, "How do we get it out?"

He laughed and removed the gold fringe that covered the top and allowed for the ornament hanger. He gently took her hand and let the ring fall into her palm. She went to put it on but he stopped her.

"Uh-uh," he shook his head. "I haven't heard and answer yet,

Ms. Miller. Will you be my bride?"

"Of course I will! Yes! Yes, a hundred times."

She leaned up to kiss him as he slid he ring on her finger.

CHAPTER TWENTY-TWO

Later that evening she snuggled against her fiancé, who wore the sweater and new watch she had given him that morning. "This feels so nice. We've made all our calls. Everyone knows and is happy for us. The ring fits perfectly, I have a job and we have a new home in Queens as of a week from now. Could we ask for anything more?" She worried slightly when his body tensed at her words. "What's wrong?" she asked, fear pooling in her belly.

He plucked a strand of her hair from her face and pushed it behind her ear. He looked sad, but how could he be sad? Everything was perfect. It had all worked out exactly as they wanted.

"Hannah, I have to ask you for one more gift."

"You know I'd give you anything."

"I do." He smiled, but the sadness lingered in his eyes. "I have everything I could ask for except one thing and I'm worried that the one thing that I need to ask of you may prove to be more than you're willing to give."

The nervous energy inside of her peaked and she sat up straight.

"Just tell me, Charles. You're scaring me. What don't you have that you need?"

"My old friend in my life."

It slowly dawned on her. He was referring to Nadia, pregnant Nadia, who had been the source of conflict, fear and almost all of the tension between them. But she was also the Nadia that had been his best friend through college. The Nadia who he had cared enough about to marry so that she could become a citizen and have the life she deserved.

"What do you mean?" She twisted the ring on her left hand. "I just need you to tell me exactly what you're asking me," Hannah said.

He sat up and folded his hands between his knees giving her a shy sideways glance. "I need to be a part of my friend's life again. I want for my wife to be a part of her life, too."

Hannah sat back. She still struggled with the fact that Nadia loved Charles and always had, but then again…on the subway that day Nadia had thanked her for saving her life. She knew the baby Nadia carried didn't belong to Charles, so it must have belonged to someone else. Was it possible Nadia had found love? "So again, Charles, for right now I need you to be very clear. What are you asking me to do?"

"I'd like you to come with me to the old apartment and take a gift for the baby. One of my oldest and dearest friends is having a baby and even though she doesn't celebrate Christmas, this would be the first time since I've met her that I haven't given her a gift. It would mean the world to me if it could be a gift from both of us, and if you would go with me."

For some strange reason, the emotion that rolled through Hannah wasn't jealously or fear, but love. She felt tears forming and knew he would misinterpret them, so she spoke quickly before he could jump to a conclusion.

"I would be happy and proud to go with you to take Nadia and her baby a present. Despite everything that's happened and the fear that I have legitimately felt over her presence in our lives, I know now that she isn't a threat. She never really was."

His shoulders sank in relief and he pulled her back towards him. He pressed his lips against her hair and mumbled, "I love you, Hannah Miller."

She shoved up off the couch.

"Let's get moving, then. She's pregnant and probably tired. I doubt she'll be up until all hours."

"You're amazing, Hannah. Let me just run and get the gift. Grab your coat!"

Her words hung in the air, "She's pregnant and probably tired." She yawned and lifted the silver framed photo. November 28. Today was Dec. 25. Had it been a whole month since their first night in Ohio together? How could she not have noticed?

Charles appeared in his coat, holding his hat and gloves. She tried to put herself in his place. If it had been her friend and she had gone through everything that Nadia and he had together, there was no way she could have abandoned them. She was proud and relieved that she loved a man of integrity.

"Oops," he said and turned around. He ran back to the bedroom again and came carrying a gift wrapped in yellow paper with small giraffes printed on it.

"When did you get that? I didn't even notice it."

"It was under the bed. Truth?" he asked.

"Always truth," she answered.

"I bought it the day after I found out she was pregnant. I was just standing outside of Macys and I had to go in. Have you ever shopped in the baby department before, Hannah? Who knew there was so much stuff that a kid could need?"

She laughed at his innocence and ignorance, "Yeah, who knew?" she replied, wondering if she, herself, might need to know sooner than she thought.

***

Early the next morning Hannah snuck out of bed, careful not to wake her snoring fiancé. Tiptoeing into the living area she grabbed her purse and pulled out the pregnancy test she'd picked up on the way home from Nadia's the night before. It had been a good thing that they were out of milk, and that Charles had agreed to let her run in alone. She didn't want to get his hopes up for something that was probably not that likely.

She'd gone off the pill when she'd come home from New York because she didn't want to make sleeping with any of her new suitors too easy, and it seemed smart to have to ask them to wear a condom, not that she'd gotten past first base with any of them. With Charles though, they hadn't always been as careful as they should have. Sitting in the bathroom waiting for the plus or minus to appear she let her hopes get the better of her. There was really no reason not to be excited. They were taking giant leaps together anyway. What was one more?

A knock sounded on the door.

"You in there? Hurry up. I've gotta go."

"Just a second," she said knowing that it would literally be just a second before she knew the truth.

She picked the test up from the counter and let out a small squeal at the confirmation of baby McMillan's impending arrival.

"You OK? Do you need help?" He called from the other side of the door.

She looked at the test in her hand and didn't know what to do. She didn't want this to be the way he found out he was going to be a father.

"I'm fine, just dropped my hairbrush in the toilet," she answered. "I'll be out in just a sec." She quickly turned on the water and ran her brush under the stream. Taking toilet paper off the roll, she wrapped the test so that it couldn't be seen and placed it in the trash. Good enough, she thought.

Striving for calm, she opened the door and pushed passed him, even faking a yawn and pretending she couldn't wait to get back into bed. He shut the door and she screamed into a pillow. How was she supposed to go back to sleep with news like this to share? Her heart was beating a mile a minute, still she found a way to climb back under the covers and wait for him to join her.

When he returned he scooted up against her and wrapped her in his arms.

"I love you," he mumbled.

"Hmmm…" she answered trying to pretend she wasn't wide-awake.

"I wanted to thank you again for going last night." He pressed his lips to the back of her head as he spooned her. "It really means a lot for me to still have Nadia, and now her new boyfriend and child in my life. I can't believe she's really going to be a mom."

"Me either," she said, wondering why he was feeling so chatty when he normally would roll over and go back to sleep.

"You know," he kept talking, "Seeing her pregnant last night made me really happy that you and I have this time with each other before we have kids. I've always believed it's really important for people to establish who they are as a couple before they start a family."

She felt her breathing hitch. She wouldn't cry.

"You have?"

"Definitely," he said as he nuzzled her neck. "Of course, that was before I found this pregnancy test in the trash and got the greatest news of my life."

Holding the test in one hand, he pulled her around to face him.

"Oh, no! I'm so sorry Hannah! I was teasing you." He bent and kissed the tear from her cheek. "I found the test so I thought I'd tease you. I'm happy, I promise. I've never been happier in my entire life."

"Really?" she asked.

"Honestly."

"Well, these aren't sad tears anyway. Do you think after yesterday with the boxes and the gift card I'd actually fall for another one of your tricks. They're happy tears, hormonal – but happy."

She leaned in to kiss him.

"Uh, Hannah?"

"What now?" she asked.

"Do you think I could put this pee stick somewhere else before we get too busy celebrating?"

She laughed and crawled on top of him before taking the test from his hand and placing it on the bedside table.

He pushed her hair from her face and looked into her eyes. "I can't believe we're here. After all this time I always knew that if I could be with you, we'd fall in love and we could make it work."

She nodded and leaned down to kiss him.

"Oh yeah," she said. "No doubt. This is going to work."

The End

ABOUT THE AUTHOR

Mary Mamie Hardesty lives and works in Louisville, KY. She is an avid reader and fan of the romance genre and is thrilled to finally be a contributing member of the community. She is happy to interact with readers on Amazon or Goodreads.

www.ingramcontent.com/pod-product-compliance
Lightning Source LLC
Chambersburg PA
CBHW060429130626
46555CB00005B/2280